About the Storyweaver Series . . .

Beth captures not only the harsh realities of life for children all over the world, but also how they intersect with beautiful stories of God using his people to live out the gospel—all written in a voice ideal for preteen kids. These stories have much potential for mobilizing this generation to make a difference in the world.

—*Jenny Funderburke, Minister to Children,*
West Bradenton Baptist Church

Tales of the Not Forgotten is a masterfully woven book. Beth in her patented story-telling style connects you to the cry of the orphan throughout the world. . . . My daughter now understands better what it mean to "look after orphans and widows."

—*Curtis Cecil, father of six, two adopted*

Beth is one of the most anointed ministers of the gospel I know. Her powerful storytelling leaves you—and your preteens—feeling emboldened to take part in how God is moving in the world.

—*Evan Doyle, Communication Specialist,*
KidzMatter, Inc.

One of the highlights of my year was getting to know Beth and to get to see and hear her heart for God and his kids around the world. I'm excited about this new book and how God is defending the orphan. Make sure you read *Tales of the Not Forgotten*—it's a game changer!

—*Jim Wideman, children's ministry pioneer,*
Jim Wideman Ministries

This book changed my daughter's life—she was brought to tears reading the stories of the children. Her teacher stated that she can tell this book changed Ceili.

—*Chelle Lynn, reader*

I was truly captivated by *Tales of the Not Forgotten*. Beth places the reader right there beside the characters as they go through their pain and turmoil, and eventually experience the touch of our great Lord's hand. This book tugs at your heart, prompts you to do more, and demonstrates that God will never leave us, nor forsake us (Hebrews 13:5).

—*Amy Tuell, Mission Team Leader*

This book has provided a graspable path for my children to be exposed to the needs of kids around the globe. Together we praise God for what he is doing and ask, how can we help?

> —Krista Regan, mama of two boys who love Jesus

The Storyweaver series reminds us all that nothing happens by accident. These stories are living proof that every act of kindness is part of God's master plan. They inspire us to look twice, extend a hand, offer a smile—you never know when the Storyweaver will use us to change others' lives, or use them to change ours.

> —Tina Rogal, sponsor mom of kids in Mexico and Africa

The Storyweaver series helped me to see that the face of Jesus is a child I have never met, in a place I may never go to, hurting in a way I may never be able to fully understand. . . . These stories show just how far the arm of the Lord reaches and just how deep and wide his love is.

> —Melissa Parsons, wife, mother, and servant

Tales of the Not Forgotten is a must read because it highlights the desperate plight of the orphan around the world through gripping, true stories. 163,000,000 orphans get a voice in this work.

> —James Wendell Bush, Minister to Students,
> Rosemont Baptist Church

Beth is a master storyteller—one of the best there is anywhere in the contemporary church—to which any of the tens-of-thousands who have heard her speak can attest. As cohost of our national radio show, *Real Life, Real Talk*, I have the joy of hearing these stories every week. . . . In *Tales of the Not Forgotten* she transports readers through her personal and heartfelt style into the gripping stories that mark Back2Back's labor of love among orphans and impoverished people around the world. Once I read *Tales* I invariably found myself talking to everyone I knew about the God-sized, compassionate, riveting, and profound stories I found inside.

> —Dr. Rob Hall, Research Analyst,
> Cincinnati Hills Christian Academy

TALES
OF
THE ONES
LED OUT

BETH GUCKENBERGER

WARNING: THESE STORIES MAY CHANGE THE WAY YOU SEE THE WORLD

Standard®
PUBLISHING

www.standardpub.com

Published by Standard Publishing, Cincinnati, Ohio
www.standardpub.com

These stories are inspired by true events and real people. In some cases, names were changed to protect identities and details of dialogue and actions were imagined. Six billion stories are unfolding daily. These are just a few.

Also available: *Tales of the Ones Led Out Leader's Guide*, 978-0-7847-7521-9, *Tales of the Defended Ones*, 978-0-7847-3697-5; *Tales of the Defended Ones Leader's Guide*, 978-0-7847-3698-2; *Tales of the Not Forgotten*, 978-0-7847-3528-2; *Tales of the Not Forgotten Leader's Guide*, 978-0-7847-3527-5.

Printed in: United States of America
Editor: Laura Derico
Cover design and illustration: Scott Ryan

All Scripture quotations, unless otherwise indicated, are taken from the HOLY BIBLE, NEW INTERNATIONAL VERSION®. NIV®. Scripture quotations marked (NLT) are taken from the Holy Bible, New Living Translation, copyright © 1996, 2004, 2007 by Tyndale House Foundation. Used by permission of Tyndale House Publishers, Inc., Carol Stream, Illinois 60188. All rights reserved. Copyright © 1973, 1978, 1984, 2011 by Biblica, Inc.™ Used by permission. All rights reserved worldwide.

ISBN 978-0-7847-7522-6

19 18 17 16 15 14   1 2 3 4 5 6 7 8 9

Storyweaver Series by Beth Guckenberger

Tales of the Not Forgotten

Tales of the Not Forgotten Leader's Guide

Tales of the Defended Ones

Tales of the Defended Ones Leader's Guide

Tales of the Ones Led Out

Tales of the Ones Led Out Leader's Guide

Other Titles by Beth Guckenberger

Relentless Hope

Reckless Faith

For my children,
who bring me great joy as they
continue to engage in God's story
for our family.

CONTENTS

INTRODUCTION: THE SHEPHERD · · · · · · · · · · · · · · 11

1 PRIYANKA'S HOPE · · · · · · · · · · · · · · · · · 19

2 ADRIAN'S SHOES · · · · · · · · · · · · · · · · · · 55

3 ANNE-MARIE'S CALL · · · · · · · · · · · · · · · 91

4 STEVE'S HOME · · · · · · · · · · · · · · · · · · · 119

5 SHANNEN'S DREAM · · · · · · · · · · · · · · · 153

6 TURNING THE PAGES · · · · · · · · · · · · · · · 189

ABOUT THIS AUTHOR · · · · · · · · · · · · · · · · · · · 199

The one who enters by the gate is the shepherd of the sheep. The gatekeeper opens the gate for him, and the sheep listen to his voice. He calls his own sheep by name and leads them out. When he has brought out all his own, he goes on ahead of them, and his sheep follow him because they know his voice.

—John 10:2-4

INTRODUCTION

THE SHEPHERD

He calls his own sheep by name and leads them out.
—John 10:3

There is a Shepherd, the one in the verse above—he is the one I call Storyweaver. He knows the path ahead, and he has a perspective higher than mine. He knows me by name. (And he knows you, too.)

He can see us all the time, in the good times and when we get in messes. If we listen, he will lead us out.

Have you ever heard him?

I remember the first time I knew he was calling me by name. I was in third grade at a church camp and the counselor had walked us up a big hill. When we got to the top, I could see crosses in the ground, and when I looked closer, I could see each one had a name on it. "These are the names of past campers who have made commitments to Christ during their week," she said.

I knew a lot about Jesus. I already knew I loved him, but I hadn't yet asked him to live in my heart.

Elizabeth, my counselor, talked to us under a tree about a shepherd who had one hundred sheep. One of those sheep got lost and, instead of staying with the other ninety-nine sheep, the shepherd left them to go out and look for the one missing. Eventually, he found the stray sheep and put it up on his shoulders. He carried it back to the others, celebrating. Elizabeth explained to us that Jesus had left everything to come and look for us.

Beth and Todd making new friends in Mexico in their new home.

Did we hear him as he was calling out our names?

I strained to listen, and then I felt something move inside me—the voice of a holy God whispering in my heart. I couldn't hear any words, but I could feel him.

I practically stood on tiptoe as I raised my hand high. "Yes, Beth?" Elizabeth asked.

"I hear him. I want a cross in this field. I want to identify with Jesus. I am lost and want to be found."

Later that evening, we walked up the hill, Elizabeth and I, with a cross bearing my name and a feeling I can't quite describe, but don't want to leave.

I have heard his voice since, sometimes in a song that says exactly what I need to hear. It might encourage me to follow through on a conversation I want to have, but am afraid to. It might convict me of an attitude that doesn't belong in the heart of one who loves the Storyweaver.

I have heard his voice coming through someone else, who echoes God's truth back to me.

I have heard him speaking through Scripture, and in the still small voice that comes when I am quiet.

I remember when my husband and I first heard

him calling us to move to Mexico. I was a teacher and the idea of being a missionary was exciting, but terrifying! I couldn't speak Spanish. I didn't know anyone from Mexico. What could God do with *me*?

I have said since that it felt like a magnet, like something was pulling us in a direction not everyone understood, but we would have to deliberately pull back from to resist. Has that ever happened to you? You thought God was leading you somewhere and, instead of following, you wanted to change directions? When we first thought God was leading us, we were afraid. Listening to God can mean sometimes he asks of us more than we are comfortable offering. He might ask us to befriend someone we think of as strange, or an enemy. Or he might ask us to start a conversation with someone who might reject us. He might ask us to share what we'd rather not, or go when we'd prefer to stay. But here's what we can be sure of: If the Shepherd, who knows us by name, asks us to go or speak or offer, it's because he can see something up ahead we can't see yet. He always has our good in mind, and we can trust that, whatever we are afraid of, God will be there.

This year, our family traveled to India, and there we met Amos and Elizabeth. They are pastors of a small church in a slum of Hyderabad, a large city in southern India. Their congregation, thirty-five families in all, are first-generation believers, sacrificing in a way I'll never understand. Deciding to follow Christ and abandon their Hindu families means a lifetime of separation from what and who they've known. Amos talked of a beating he received almost two years ago

A scene from the Hyderabad slums.

now, a result of his evangelism in a community reluctant to hear that they were once lost, but now can be found. He looked at me straight in the eye and said he would do it all over again, because what happened after that incident drew his church together, and lives were saved.

While in his home, I shared with Amos some verses on forgiveness and reconciliation, simple messages that have meant something to me. He looked grateful, but I know no matter what knowledge I had to share, he has wisdom I might not ever gain. When you listen and follow, listen and follow, not counting the cost, but only trusting the voice, the result is a faith muscle that is strong, a wisdom you can't learn, but earn.

How strong is your faith muscle? When we use it, by listening and obeying, it gets exercised. Have you ever heard of the Hebrew word *chutzpah*? It means audacity, gall, nerve. Jesus rewards the woman who won't take no for an answer after pleading with Jesus to heal her daughter (Mark 7:25-30). She showed nerve. She had chutzpah. She had faith that God would come through for her.

Have you asked anything of God?

Jesus tells us the story of the widow who won't stop knocking on the door of the judge (Luke 18:1-8). That's chutzpah. Her faith, her nerve, her persistence were rewarded. When we ask God for things boldly (Heal my sister! Give me courage! Open my friends' hearts!) and then expect him to answer—to call our names, to lead us out—we delight the heart of Jesus. We have a responsibility to tell his stories and celebrate how he moves and answers our prayers. I will share with you five stories I know, and then you think about stories you know. Maybe stories from your school or home or church, stories that celebrate a God who is listening. Stories about the Shepherd, and about the ones he led out.

POST CARD

CORRESPONDENCE

Hebrew is the language in which most of the Old Testament was recorded. Chutzpah is a Hebrew word that means having the gall to do something bold, or as we might say today, having guts.

Chutzpah means "audacity, gall."

Chapter 1
PRIYANKA'S HOPE

Another day of cleaning, another day of surviving. Amita sighed and walked slowly back to her apartment, dragging her tired body up the stairs to the rented room she shared with her daughters.

"Four daughters, bum luck." That's what everyone said. "Too bad you never had a son."

But when Amita looked at her children, she couldn't feel anything but happy. It didn't matter that everyone looked on her with pity. Some people even thought she might be cursed.

"Just look what happened," they would say. "The husband left her. Who can blame him?" In India, coming up with the dowry for four women was impossible for a poor man. There was far less shame in leaving the family than in staying and being unable to provide a dowry. So off he went, leaving Amita to care for the four girls alone.

At the top of the four flights of steps, she took a moment outside her doorway to catch her breath.

She slipped off her worn shoes and pushed aside the sheet that served as a door. Amita smiled, knowing the day would get better the minute she saw her four little angels.

Priyanka, age twelve, was waiting for her. The girl knew her mother's schedule by heart and was always ready with some news for her *amma* the moment she arrived. "Amma, guess what? I saved some extra *chapati* for you from the feeding center!" she held out the little bit of rice and some flat bread she had saved from her meal earlier that day. Grateful, Amita took the chapati and scooped up the rice, thanking the gods for this gift. As usual, she hadn't eaten much that day, and was feeling a bit lightheaded. *This might be enough to keep a headache away tonight.*

Hasiriva, just two years behind Priyanka, didn't even look up when her mother walked in. She was sitting on the ground, using the paper and pencil she'd found that day at the dump to practice the letters she was learning at the feeding center. The teacher had told her that if she learned to write and say all her letters, the teacher would give her a new backpack. Then Hasiriva knew she would feel like a real student. She stayed lost in her own thoughts as Priyanka chattered to Amma.

Supriya, eight years old, and Krupapiya, six, rounded out the little house of women. They were playing together in the corner of the room, pretending to get married, imagining themselves getting ready to perform elaborate dances with handsome suitors. Since they both wanted to wear red, they pretended their husbands were already there, and the dancing began. They paused for a moment to greet their mother, but then went right back to their ceremony. They were too young to notice the fatigue

Two Indian girls play with a red veil. Indian brides traditionally dress in red.

in their mother's step, the dirt on the floor, or the dullness of another day. Amita smiled again in the dim light of the dreary little apartment. *For a season, they are just girls. Not poor girls, not abandoned girls, not cursed girls. Just regular, make-believe-sari-swirling girls.*

Amita wanted to put her feet up, enjoy her bread, and breathe deeply in the relief that comes with being in your own space, next to the people you love. However, there was a heaviness on her heart that she could never shake. She felt her husband's absence as sharply today as she had the moment she discovered he had left her. So many nights they had spent together, alongside each other, and so many mornings they had woken up together, helping each other face the day. And then one morning he was just gone. She wasn't surprised—not really. The fights and tension and pressure had been building and building since Krupapiya's birth. Another girl, another weight around his neck. No son, no relief. How many times had Amita looked into those beautiful dark eyes of her husband and seen only shame, fear, dread? He just couldn't handle it.

Since that day, the very day he left, Amita had worked as a day maid. She had gone out right away and found work, knowing she could not depend on friends or relatives to support her family. Every day Amita thanked the gods for this position. She received about 4000 rupees per month—enough to pay the rent for their room (2000) and to feed the family of five women. After basic supplies were bought, nothing was left.

It was a great help to Amita that her daughters were able to go to the Christ

A rupee is the basic unit of Indian currency. 1 rupee = less than 2 cents for All Feeding Center. They went there every afternoon to study, have a meal, and hear about the Bible. Amita didn't know anything about the Bible, but the stories her daughters came home with were fantastic to hear. It made for good bedtime conversation—the girls would talk over each other, each one trying to remember and share the details with their mother. She could feel the strength in the stories—though for her it was a little scary to think of one god having so much power.

But Amita didn't really care much about what they learned. One god was as good as the next—none of them seemed to notice her little family much, anyway. She was just glad they were learning something good. At best, if she could come up with the fees, her girls could attend government schools and be expected to finish class 10 (10th grade). But she wasn't always able to come up with the fees, and some years the children had missed school. Now the girls were falling behind. But even if they could finish their schooling, what would that get them? They wouldn't be qualified for any kind of well-paying job. They would be destined to work in a job like hers—using their bodies and not their minds. With no qualifications and no dowry, the girls would work hard on their own for the rest of their lives.

Amita's eyes passed from one face to the other around the room. The last bit of sunlight had gone and the girls were settled on their mats for the night. With some effort she raised herself out of her chair and went to each mat, pulling up a blanket on the little girls, slipping the pencil out of Hasiriva's sleepy grasp, and smoothing Priyanka's hair. *I wonder if they know these are the best years of their lives.*

Colorful images of Hindu gods adorn the temples in India.

Madhapaul was a blessed man. He learned of Jesus early on in life and now walked among the 1 billion Indians who don't know the Savior God. He had always wondered what his calling was—what could he do for his people? In response to his own questions and God's guidance, he had spent years building a Christian school, a sterling reputation, and a strong family. Now, well into adulthood, he realized he still wanted more. He asked the Lord, *How can I be used? Do you want to use my story? my school? my family?* He struggled to understand God's plan for his life. But as he asked these questions, he felt certain that he wanted to build more than just his own little kingdom in his own life. Madhapaul wanted to help build God's kingdom!

One day as he was puzzling out what all this meant, his eyes came to rest once again on a familiar Bible passage: "The gatekeeper opens the gate for him, and the sheep listen to his voice. He calls his own sheep by name and leads them out" (John 10:3). *That's it!* He wanted to join Jesus in this leading-out business. As he prayed and listened, he heard a whisper to return home.

It was a Tuesday, and the afternoon started out like all others at the feeding center. There were songs and games, a story and a meal, but Priyanka knew today was different. She had been feeling something inside her, something she couldn't quite explain. She tried to describe it to a volunteer.

The woman listened patiently and then offered, "It sounds like what you are feeling is expectation . . . or anticipation? Or maybe you would call it hope? If you could hope for anything, what would you hope for?"

Priyanka let those questions roll around in her head. Expectation? As the oldest of four sisters, what she expected was more responsibility. She could feel it coming. Many girls her age and younger had taken jobs already. She wasn't blind—she knew her mother had shielded her from that so far. But she could also see the worn lines in her mother's face, and that her steps were getting slower. Priyanka tried to do her duty and take care of their little household as best as she could. She woke her sisters each morning (most days her mother left very early, while it was still dark) and made sure they all got dressed and completed their few household chores: sweeping the floor, pulling the mats neatly against the

INDIA

wall, preparing a small amount of lentils and rice for a meal later.

She knew, however, she would need to do more if they were going to survive and be able to stay in their home together. One week last year her mother had become very sick. Priyanka remembered the feeling of panic—what would they do if she did not get well? They could not pay for doctors or medicines. What about when it came time to pay the rent? In the end, somehow it had all worked out—the girls were able to go to the feeding center while their mother rested, and they brought back soup for her that made her feel better. But Priyanka knew her family's security was a day-to-day struggle. Lately she had thought often about dropping out of her classes and taking on a job—perhaps working as a maid, like her mother. She knew as a fatherless girl in a lower caste family, this was where she would end up. Not swirling in red at her wedding, as her little sisters dreamed about. Priyanka had given up these fantasies—reality stared her in the face.

So why did these questions press so hard into her heart? Why did she keep feeling so jumpy—like something big was coming? She felt confused. *If I could hope for anything . . . What was there to hope for?*

Madhapaul obeyed the still, small voice he had heard and returned to the humble village where he was raised. To the people there, he looked like a king—with a car and nice clothes and a story about how he had built a school. There were many who congratulated him and bowed before him, telling him he was favored by the gods. Madhapaul felt the temptation to take credit—to tell everyone about how he worked hard in school and then after school, how he made his own way—or even to just accept their explanations about the gods. But he knew in his heart that all that he had and who he had become was due to the Lord. None of it could have happened by his own power. So he tried to tell the people his story and what had happened to him in the light of the Messiah, sprinkling in the spiritual truths he had come to cherish.

But the people who had gathered around soon tired of hearing his stories, and they started to share their own. Many of the stories were about the frustrations of village life. Some asked Madhapaul for jobs. One man began loudly lamenting his son's inability to find a suitable wife. Madhapaul innocently asked why this was such a problem—when he was a boy he remembered many girls living in the village. As the man's tales unfolded, Madhapaul's skin crawled. There were stories of girls being made to work in the fields at very young ages. And worse still, uneducated tribal girls being sold into slavery.

"What use are girls? They can't bring honor to your family!"

"Girls can't work hard enough to be worth anything."

"Girls are expensive—you pay for them to grow up and then you have to pay a dowry just for them to go and be married and live somewhere else."

"The worst part about daughters is they can't be sons."

The voices of many men grumbled over the problem of these unwanted creatures. The only easy solution, they said, was to find the slave trader, receive the going rate of 2000 rupees, and let the girls be shipped off to Mumbai. Problem solved.

Amita heaved her pack of cleaning supplies and tools up the few steps to get on the bus that would take her home. Another maid helped her up—she knew how a person's legs felt like heavy bags of grain after twelve hours of work, mostly standing. Once in her seat, Amita just turned and stared out the window. She didn't have the energy to talk today. As the images passing by changed from shiny office towers and well-landscaped apartment complexes to the dirty, crowded streets of the slums, Amita felt the weight of her worries bearing down on her shoulders.

While she was at work, she didn't have to think about her life, or the lives of her girls. She liked to focus on the tasks at hand. Shining faucets, cleaning floors, doing laundry, even dealing with harsh bosses—it was all hard work. But it was harder to come home to those girls' faces and wonder what they would eat this week. They were growing so fast—how could she ever buy new clothes for them? Priyanka was getting older; she could get a job now. The extra money

The apartment houses of a typical Indian city.

could help, but what about her education? Four girls. One little room. So many problems.

She watched the faces that passed by outside. The bus went through some of the worst parts of the city—the parts the people in the shiny towers didn't want to see or hear or smell. She watched for the faces of women—women working in the filth of the streets. Young girls begging. Women selling scraps of food, of cloth . . . themselves.

Amita closed her eyes and rubbed her forehead. Her head was beginning to ache. Afraid of causing ill will with her thoughts, she thanked the gods for what she had—a place of her own to come home to, their own bathroom (something of a luxury where they lived), a job, her girls. *It could be worse*, she thought. *These women in the streets have nothing.* The thought of Priyanka getting a job came to her again. *These women have no hope. But what hope can I really offer my daughters?*

Girls being sold? What for? As Madhapaul walked around the village, asking questions and listening to stories, his stomach churned. *This isn't right. These stories are full of darkness: poor living conditions, forced labor, ashrams and slaves . . . These people are being sold a lie, or maybe they just don't care.* He knew the girls that were sold were not getting the shelter and education their families were promised. He suspected the families knew it too, but just decided it was a better fate than they could offer. Plus, they didn't want to turn down that much money.

All night long, Madhapaul tossed and turned on his mat. He could see the faces of the girls he grew up with, and he realized he didn't know where most of them were now. *Were they sold? Where are they now? Do they have schooling and families and houses and happy lives? Or are their lives filled with this darkness?* Madhapaul prayed over and over, *Lord, who will take care of these village girls? Is this what you brought me here to see? They cannot go with the slave traders. Who will take care of these girls?* His mind floated back to the birth of his own daughter and the joy his family experienced as a result of her life. *Who will take care of these daughters?*

The words of Psalm 139 came to his mind as he was praying: "Even the darkness will not be dark to you" (v. 12). He wondered if these girls could be made to understand how beautiful and wonderful they were. And how much they were worth to God.

In the morning, he knew what to do. He didn't know exactly how to do it, but he would take them—the village girls who were not wanted. He would take them with him to the city, to live at his school and begin their education. How would he feed them? What would they wear? Who would take care of them? These things he did not know. But he knew that the moment he raised his hand to the Lord, he felt a peace—a tremendous green-light peace. *Step out, Madhapaul!* It was as if God was speaking directly to him.

If I go up to the heavens, you are there; if I make my bed in the depths, you are there. If I rise on the wings of the dawn, if I settle on the far side of the sea, even there your hand will guide me, your right hand will hold me fast. If I say, "Surely the darkness will hide me and the light become night around me," even the darkness will not be dark to you; the night will shine like the day, for darkness is as light to you. For you created my inmost being; you knit me together in my mother's womb. I praise you because I am fearfully and wonderfully made; your works are wonderful, I know that full well. My frame was not hidden from you when I was made in the secret place. When I was woven together in the depths of the earth, your eyes saw my unformed body. All the days ordained for me were written in your book before one of them came to be.

—Psalm 139:8-16

Priyanka stood at the end of the line at the feeding center like she did every week. She waited till everyone else was fed so she could ask her question quietly: Was there anything left over she could take home to her mother? Sometimes the volunteer serving the meal could answer yes, but most days it was no—every last crumb was eaten. But just the chance that the answer might be yes was enough to keep Priyanka asking each week.

Today the volunteer scraped the last bits of rice and vegetable curry into a small bag and handed it to Priyanka. As she did so, she noticed the sadness in Priyanka's eyes. But this volunteer was new at the center—having only volunteered once before. She didn't know if she should talk to the girl herself or get someone else. But she felt someone ought to reach

POST CARD

PON ENCE

Ashrams are a place of spiritual retreat for Hindus.

out to this little, clearly hurting girl. She looked out into the sea of children who had gathered there this afternoon, eating what, for many of them, would be their only meal that day. *How many more like her are there?* It seemed overwhelming, but the volunteer figured that God must have made her notice this little girl's dark eyes for a reason. She finished up the dishes and set out to look for Goldie, the director of the center. Goldie would know just what to do.

Children receiving a meal at the feeding center.

"That little girl, Priyanka, I don't know . . . She seems sad tonight, almost heavy. She needs someone to talk to, and I don't know what to say to her." Goldie listened patiently and smiled. It was a familiar report from new volunteers. It was easy to sense the weight of the story lines of these children—every single one of them came from a challenging background of one kind or another. Volunteers were often struck by the sorrow that these little ones seemed to bear—and there was not always time to tend to every heart in a day. Nevertheless, Goldie followed the prompting and, praying silently for the words to say, walked over to Priyanka.

It is believed that up to 35 million children in India are orphans, and of those, 3 million live in the streets.

Priyanka looked up from the game her sisters were playing when she heard Goldie's voice. "Would you like to sit for a moment with me?" She nodded her reply and went with the kind lady. Priyanka always wished Goldie could be her aunt. They had been cut off from most of their family when their father left them. Priyanka had cloudy memories of aunts and uncles and an older woman—perhaps a grandmother? But she had not spoken of them for a long time, and her mother never talked about them. Priyanka guessed it would be too sad for her.

The sun was setting. Normally by this time Priyanka would be gathering her sisters up for the walk home. But she wasn't ready to leave the feeding center yet this evening. For just a little while longer, she wanted to stay where she felt safe and at ease, and put off the responsibility that would shift onto her shoulders once they walked out the door.

The older woman sat with the girl for a moment in silence. Then she said, "Look up at the sky over there. Do you see the moon coming out?"

Priyanka nodded. It was faint, but she could just make out the shape of a crescent moon.

Goldie continued, "See how you can only see part of it, but your mind tells you there is more there?"

Priyanka kept looking in the sky, and whispered, "*Haan*." She could see it.

"I think that's a word picture for what the Lord wants to tell you tonight. You can only see a part of this story line you are in, and so you worry. You don't know what will happen to you, to your mother, to your sisters, in your future . . . But, your mind's eye is telling you there is more there, more coming. And it's going to be good." Goldie watched Priyanka's eyes sparkle and dance in the moonlight. The girl sat very still, with her face turned up to the sky. Then she shut her eyes.

Goldie's voice dropped to almost a whisper. "I think God is talking to you. He is telling you something, isn't he? He is revealing himself to you for the first time. That's the pricking you are feeling in your heart. That's why you feel nervous and confused. His Spirit is stirring in you."

POST CARD

CORRESPONDENCE

Haan means "Yes."

Priyanka opened her eyes again. Her breathing, once quick and shallow, became more rhythmic and deep. Goldie pressed on, "Do you believe in the God we teach about here? The one who slays giants and feeds children? The one who died on the cross for you? Do you believe in what he has for you? Do you hear him calling your name?"

A holy, eternal, sovereign God was whispering to a lost, abandoned, Indian girl of low caste—worthless in the eyes of her world. But all of Heaven was waiting to hear her speak . . .

All the families came from Hindu backgrounds, so they wouldn't understand the man's story of a restless night wrestling with a God who wants to offer something for nothing. But that was OK. Madhapaul knew the people would trust him because they knew him—he was from their village. And faith in him could be a first step to faith in something much bigger than him.

The girls gathered in little nervous clusters as the departure time came. Some of them were sad to leave their families, and all of them were scared of leaving the world they knew. They didn't realize they were quite literally walking away from the chains that were meant to bind them. They listened respectfully as this man (who seemed quite wealthy to them) told them about education, and shelter, and about a teacher named Jesus, who died for them. But they didn't really understand what he was talking about. However, when he passed out good food for them and spoke kindly to them, they smiled broadly and laughed. They knew they were safe with him.

After the initial exodus of twenty-five girls, Madhapaul went back again for another twenty-five, and then again, until he had sixty-nine girls from his village and twenty-one from surrounding areas. His wife had great faith and encouraged him to keep listening and obeying. They read about Mother Teresa and were inspired by her faith. They hung part of a quotation from her up in their home: "I am a little pencil in God's hands."

Priyanka's eyes filled with tears. She couldn't find her voice, so she just nodded.

"Do you believe what God writes for you is good? That his stories are not just for other people, but that he is writing a story right now for you and Hasiriva and Supriya and Krupapiya and your mom? Do you believe that his stories for your family are good?"

Priyanka's head nodded more vigorously now. Then she tilted her head to one side, and looked

I am a little pencil in God's hands. He does the thinking. He does the writing. He does everything and sometimes it is really hard because it is a broken pencil and he has to sharpen it a little more. Be a little instrument in his hands so that he can use you anytime, anywhere. We have only to say "yes" to God.

—Mother Teresa, *The Joy in Loving*

straight at Goldie. She asked, "What about my dad? I remember him. I remember when he left. I put my faith in him and he failed us." Priyanka looked away, over to where her two younger sisters were playing. "You say this God is my Father. But is he a father like that? Can he have a story for my dad too? And can it be good?"

Goldie collected her thoughts. Those were good questions, and not easy to answer. She started out, "Look back at the moon. God asks us to trust what we can only see in part, believing in the One who has the full story. He knows where your dad is, he knows what he is learning, and how he is struggling or growing. I don't know that your dad will come back, but if anyone can bring him back to your family, it would be this God. This one and only true God. Allow his peace to spread through you, through your family, and through your next steps. The coming chapters are good. Inside, I think you know there is more to your story. Would you like to start this next chapter? Would you like to start it as the chosen daughter of a heavenly King?"

Priyanka just hugged Goldie, hanging on and feeling grateful. Later that night, when she would stare at the moon from the balcony of her family's room, she would thank Goldie silently for the word picture she could be reminded of every night. But she wanted her sisters to see, to believe, to feel the peace—oh my goodness, the peace!—that had slipped into her heart and mind in the last few minutes. She jumped off the bench and said, "Don't move. Please! I want my sisters to hear about this God. They know the stories, but I don't think they understand he wants to put them inside of the stories. I think they believe the stories are only for other people—like cars, or daddies, or nice clothes and big houses. Will you explain it to them like you did to me? That anyone can know this God and be his daughter? That he has more for us than we can see?"

Of course Goldie would tell them; that's the very reason she opened the feeding center, to have conversations just like this one. While Priyanka gathered up her sisters, Goldie called over the volunteer who had noticed Priyanka's heaviness. She invited her into this sacred moment. "I want to share with you why God stirred your heart, and why you are here. He wants to write you into the lives of children whose names you don't even know and whose lives you could never imagine. There is a whole sea of children, yes. But your story starts always with just the one in front of you. The one he leads you to. Come with me, and let's invite these little sisters into his kingdom."

Later that hour, all four sisters placed their trust in a God they could only see right now in part. Immediately the Spirit inside of them began to bubble up, as they spoke with joy and hope of the things to come. They used the only words they knew to describe the spiritual realm they were encountering—words like "light" and "happy" and "safe" and "free."

What will our mother think? Priyanka wondered on her way home, shepherding her sisters hurriedly through the now-darkened streets. *Will she understand? Will she want to believe too? Will she be upset or angry?*

Slowly, the girls in Madhapaul's school began learning math and how to read. They heard about India's rich history and the history of God's people. It was all so new to them, but they were eager to do well.

Even though Madhapaul knew the girls had been given away—some of them even sold—many of the girls themselves didn't realize that. He encouraged them to stay in contact with their parents. It was his hope that, with education, the families would see the girls as more valuable. He knew there was always the possibility that his plan might backfire—that with their increased education, the girls might be viewed as a threat by their families, or possibly as just a ticket to a better life. But those were problems for another day. Today, he would encourage ongoing connections. He prayed for God to bless these efforts.

Every time Madhapaul went back to talk to someone in the village, they asked him how many more girls he would take. Families shoved their girls at him as he walked by, begging him to take them away. Some days the responsibility was staggering. *I can't do this alone. I need more help.*

Madhapaul stared up at the moon one night, wondering about all the Indian children who might be sleeping under that same moon. *How many of them have families? How many of them are alone? How many of them can I help?* He prayed for the girls in his school, and for their teachers. And he prayed for Indian girls everywhere in the city, and for those who were teaching them, taking care of them, leading them.

After several weeks, the girls began to open up. They asked questions about how Jesus fit in with the Hindu lifestyle they had always known. They learned songs, committed verses to memory, and practiced saying names such as Abraham, Moses, and Noah. They had a service every Saturday and three directed prayer times a day. The Spirit was in pursuit of these lives and the campaign to win their hearts was going strong.

Priyanka led her sisters home the same way she had a hundred times before, but nothing felt the same. They practically danced up the stairs and into the apartment, knowing they had a few more hours to wait until their mom arrived. They immediately began planning how they would tell her what happened, deciding that Priyanka should speak first.

Later that night, Amma finally arrived home. She barely had time to slip off her shoes and uncover her head before her daughters all gathered around, bright-eyed and obviously waiting to tell her

From Beth's Journal

This is a story not over yet, a story of God raising up a new generation of young women in a country full of people who don't understand his ways. God is our Storyweaver. He knows if the dad will return, if the mother will find peace, if the children will hold on to hope. He knows how to encourage the volunteers, like Goldie and Madhapaul, who work in Indian slums and among lives considered worth only the money paid by slave traders. He knows each one and he calls them by name. Who will listen to him?

something. "Now what's this all about?" she asked. She smiled at their eagerness, but she couldn't help thinking to herself, *And how much will it cost?*

She listened to their stories and took note of the joy in their faces. But when the girls gathered that night in prayer, she did not join them. The girls were disappointed. Some hid it better than others.

"Just pray, Amma!" Krupapiya blurted out. "You will have a new life! Don't you want a new life?"

A new life? Amita sighed heavily as she laid down on her mat. *I want my old life back. With my husband, and family, and plans and dreams. I want my time back—when I didn't have to work so hard.*

Priyanka saw her mom's face and her heart sank. She tried pleading. "Maybe God will bring Pita back! Have you ever thought of that? Maybe this God who can split seas and raise people from the dead, maybe he can find Daddy, and tell him where we are!" She fell into her mother's arms, sobbing. "Please, just believe. Pray with us."

Amita cried with her daughter, but for different reasons. She cried because she didn't understand how she felt, and she didn't like feeling this deeply. She cried because her oldest daughter was taking the leadership in the family—a sign she was getting older and things would start to change. She cried because these girls didn't know the lengths she had gone to just to keep food on the table; and she cried because if they had known, they would realize no holy God would want her. These thoughts and a million more came unbidden into her mind that night. She fell into a restless sleep, still holding Priyanka in her arms, like she did when she was just a baby.

The girls in Madhapaul's home, bit by bit, grew in their understanding of Jesus. They saw Jesus as their rescuer. When they went home on school breaks, they began to realize the rejection of their families. They understood the cost of that rejection—the price they paid for being poor girls from poor families. Jesus literally led them out of their homes—out of slavery, out of lives without education. But most important, he led them out of lives without him. Madhapaul had been the pencil, but it was Jesus who was writing the stories of these girls.

And it will be Jesus who will bring more help, who will walk with these girls as they become young, professional women. And it will be Jesus who will give them words to explain their faith.

It will be and always has been him.

Priyanka waited until her mother left in the morning to bring up the conversation with her sisters again. "Girls, how do you feel this morning? I mean, after what we talked about yesterday? I know how I feel—light and happy. I feel like I'm so full of hope . . . I don't know what to do!" Hasiriva nodded and the littler girls laughed. "Well, that's all the evidence I need that this God is real. I have never woken up like this before. I think Goldie would say we just have to keep believing. Let's just keep praying for Amma to be written into this story. Let's just keep loving her and sharing with her what we learn every day. Like Goldie said yesterday, the coming chapters are good. We just have to keep listening for God to tell us what to do."

Priyanka walked out on the balcony to hang out the little, worn rug she had just washed. She looked up and saw that, even though the sun's glow had already begun to lighten the sky, she could still make out the faint shape of the moon.

She walked back in to join her sisters and smiled a big, thankful smile. "Let's pray now."

Hebrews 11:1 says, "Now faith is confidence in what we hope for and assurance about what we do not see." In this story, Priyanka was asked to look up and realize there was more to the moon than what she could see. What do you think about this? How does this story help you think about what it means to believe in God?

Priyanka and her sisters prayed for their mother to know God, just as Goldie and Madhapaul had prayed for the children in their care to know their heavenly Father. Why do you think it is good to pray for others? What happens when you pray for someone on a regular basis? Write your thoughts here.

Chapter 2

ADRIAN'S SHOES

Adrian woke up abruptly and lifted his head to do a quick check. *Still sleeping—good.* He flopped back onto his mat and looked over at the clock. 5:30 a.m. *Fifteen more minutes of quiet left before the boys' dorm becomes a tornado of activity. Chores, change clothes, breakfast, devotionals, make bed, brush teeth, check backpack, comb hair, and finally off to school.*

Adrian spent those fifteen minutes thinking over the day ahead, and worrying. As the oldest of three brothers, he couldn't help himself. He had checked on his brothers since they were born. Living in a children's home with adult guardians all around didn't change the fact that he felt responsible for them. *Did Mateo finish his math homework? Does Felipe have a clean shirt?*

The moment the wake-up bell sounded, Adrian jumped up and rushed through his duties. This was his routine—always trying to get his tasks done quickly so he could guide his brothers through theirs. But some days there just wasn't enough time—off they'd head to school, hair disheveled and shoes on the wrong feet.

His *encargada* would always tell him it was her job to take care of these details, not his, but old habits die hard. Besides, it seemed like she had too many heads to count to be able to pay attention to them all. Adrian had taken care of his brothers for a long time while his parents had focused on their jobs, their addictions, and their failing marriage. He had had a system for all the essentials—making sure everyone ate and slept and stayed relatively clean. But the school part was a problem. Back then it was hit or miss, and most days he just couldn't figure out how to get them all there on time, if at all.

That's how they had ended up here.

A schoolteacher had become concerned about the boys. She'd noticed how often they were absent, and how, when they were there, they often had trouble focusing. After catching glimpses of bruises

GUATEMALA

Guatemala City

on Adrian's arms on several different occasions, she finally told the principal, who cared enough to check in on the home. Finding signs of abuse and neglect, the principal notified a social worker. The government decided it was better for the boys to live in this orphanage than alongside two adults who were not ever there. Adrian was pretty sure he agreed with them, but some days he had his doubts.

His first impression of the orphanage was that he couldn't believe how many adults worked there. He was amazed at how quickly they learned the boys' names. Those adults were with them all the time, shuttling them between doctor's appointments, church services, and tutoring classes. Pretty soon, the boys' minds, souls, and bodies were catching up with everyone else's. For two years, things were fantastic.

POST CARD

CORRESPONDENCE

Spanish is the primary language of people who live in Central and South American countries, such as Guatemala. Five hundred million people speak Spanish around the world.

Encargada means "caretaker."

In Adrian's orphanage, 150 children live, each with a story. It costs more than $100 each month to allow the children's home to provide food, housing, clothing, health care, educational opportunities, spiritual training, and personal development for one child.

Have we really been here two whole years?

Adrian couldn't believe it, but he knew that was right. He had been just eight years old when they came—now he was ten. He was thinking this over when a door opened in front of him and a voice interrupted: "Adrian, can you come in here for a moment?"

He always loved it when Corina called him to her office. It usually meant a trip off campus—to see the dentist or to pick up a donation. Adrian never cared where they went, he just liked seeing different parts of the city. This time, however, he could tell from her face something was wrong. When he entered the room, a woman he had never seen before was sitting on the couch. Well-honed survival bells started going off inside his head, but nothing could have prepared him for what Corina was going to say.

"This is our area's social worker, Elena. She has been telling me about your parents." Adrian said nothing, but questions were shooting off in his brain like firecrackers: *Where were they? Were they dead? Dying?* Corina continued gently, "She says that your parents are doing much better! Isn't that great news?" Adrian kept his eyes focused on the tile floor, but he could feel the orphanage director looking at him.

"Sí," Adrian replied. He glanced up at her and saw her smiling at him. But the smile wasn't in her eyes. He wondered if she was playing some kind of trick on him—but that wasn't like her.

"Elena wants to take you back to your neighborhood, to your home. She can take you today. Go and gather up your brothers and tell them to fill their backpacks with their favorite things." Adrian just stood there, staring at her in disbelief. She put a hand on his shoulder. "We will miss you, but it's time for you to go home."

POST CARD

CORRESPONDENCE

En casa means "at home."

As he packed up his own bag back in the dorm, Adrian kept quiet. His brothers chattered away excitedly as they stuffed things in their packs. They were so much younger when they had last been at home. *En casa? Where is that?* Adrian could picture the room he had shared with his parents just a few years back, but he certainly never felt at home there. *What made anyone think this time would be different? Why is Corina allowing this to happen to us?*

But by the end of the day, they were back in their home, with their parents. Awkward hugs were exchanged. Their mother smiled and their father asked the boys questions as they ate dinner together.

Due to many factors (including a long civil war, natural disasters, and the rise of drug-related crime), Guatemala is the second poorest country in the Western Hemisphere, after Haiti. About 2/3 of all Guatemalan children live in poverty.

But Adrian only wanted to go to his bed.

The first few days were not so bad, though Adrian missed the structure and routine of the children's home. His parents seemed like they were trying to make things work, and he tried to be hopeful. But as the week went on, any hope of things being different this time around had disappeared. The temporary job his father had been working at ended, and he didn't seem interested in finding another. Weeks passed, and Adrian could tell his parents were using drugs and alcohol again, though they tried to hide it. Strangers were coming in and out of their house at odd times of day. More often than not, the boys came home from school (if they made it to school) to an empty house—and an empty refrigerator.

The whole next year was terrible. Adrian and his brothers were hungry all the time. There were many lonely nights and missed days of school when one or more of them was either too sick or too tired to get ready, and no parents were around to take care of them.

Adrian found himself thinking about the orphanage more and more. He even missed the busy, early mornings. Sometimes it had been hard to follow rules and keep up with the schedule, but at least it had been consistent, dependable. At the children's home, he had always known that they would eat, that they would go to school, and that, on his way out, his encargada would remind him that he could do it.

Who dreams of returning to an orphanage? Adrian asked himself.

Melanie drove to work, eating the same breakfast on the way as she did every morning. She parked in the same spot and entered the same doors to the same job she had yesterday and last week and last month and last year. But as she walked down the hallway to her desk, new thoughts were running around in her mind.

Is this all there is, Lord? Is this job what your wonderful plan is for me? I will work at it, believing I honor you, but I feel like there is something else, still another assignment. I don't know where or how or when or with whom, but I am listening. I am ready.

Lead me.

Rainy season came and went. One of Adrian's brothers had severe tooth pain and Adrian knew his parents were incapable of even addressing it. Having been left alone one too many nights with Mateo crying, Adrian

came to a new resolution. This was not a long-term solution for them. As his brother's crying turned to whimpering and then to snoring, ten-year-old Adrian made a big decision. *That's it. No more. Tomorrow I will find someone who will listen.*

In the morning he woke up and looked around the room. A pile of soiled clothes filled up one corner. His brothers were still asleep, squished together on a small mat on the floor. This was the place they had called home for the last year, but there really wasn't any room for them in this space or in the lives of their parents. Deep sadness crept into Adrian's heart. He was old enough to know not all families were like this.

The boys groggily followed his directions to pack up what they could carry. They were used to doing whatever their big brother told them to do. Adrian checked around one more time and then shut the door behind them. He had thought about leaving a note, but then decided not to bother. He knew it would be days before his parents even realized they were gone.

A sense of responsibility pushed him through the doors and into the office of the most adult, boss-like person he could find in the school. "My name is Adrian. These are my brothers, Mateo and Felipe. We are students here in this school. I need you to call Corina at Cristo Te Ama Orphanage and tell her we are waiting here until she comes to pick us up." He sounded more confident than he felt. "We will sit outside this office until she comes."

The school principal had been watching the poor performance and even worse attendance of these boys all year. She knew where the boys had come from and could see where they were headed. She knelt down and showed Adrian a bit of tenderness. "Well, a young man with your determination should be rewarded. I will do as you ask, although I can't influence what she will do." Adrian nodded. He knew Corina. He knew she would come for him.

To this day Adrian does not know or understand all the calls that were made, paperwork that was filed, favors that were asked, and steps that were taken on their behalf. The Storyweaver was working for them as he led them out of a dark place and into the next chapter of their lives.

Listening to the radio at her desk, Melanie heard a story about a World Vision sponsor. She teared up at the testimony about an American family and a boy they sponsored in Sri Lanka. *I don't even know where Sri Lanka is,* she thought. *I need to realize that this world is bigger than Hendersonville.* She couldn't help but notice how she had been drawn to international news stories lately, or to testimonies that involved overseas trips and foreign languages. *Maybe the assignment I am itching for is somewhere out there in the world? Maybe God is preparing me for something I can't even imagine.*

The first day back in the old school for Adrian was bittersweet. He loved the feel of books under his arm. He loved seeing old friends and, for a few hours, knowing everyone was safe in someone else's care.

But each time the teacher talked, he felt anxious. He didn't know what she was talking about; he hadn't realized he had fallen so far behind. He came home from school that first day angry. Angry at his parents for not caring, angry at his former school for not teaching him better, and angry at his brothers for taking up so much of his time. He was simply angry with everyone. The emotions he had held in check for years came out in a rush, and although those in his immediate environment didn't deserve his wrath, he felt he couldn't help himself.

He didn't know that the abuse and neglect he had endured from his own parents had slowly burned a wound in his heart. And now, each time someone made an unkind comment or rubbed him the wrong way, or even just asked of him more than he was able to do at the time, they touched that wound. And Adrian, feeling the pain, exploded.

Then he just felt angry at himself. *What have I done, bringing us back here? I've just made things worse! At least at home, no one expected anything of us. Am I supposed to be perfect? Do I have to remember exactly what to do, all the time? Remember these Bible verses, remember how to behave in class, remember my chores in the dorm. Remember, remember, remember! But I just want to forget.*

"And remember, you don't have to be an expert to go on a trip, or raise money for clean water, or pray or sponsor a child." Melanie's head snapped up. That was the third time that week she had heard about child sponsorship.

This is getting ridiculous! she thought, as she felt her heart pounding.

The pastor went on. "If you are interested in hearing more from our church missionary about her ministry in Guatemala, then join us this evening for coffee and cookies and a short presentation about how you can be involved." Melanie made a note about the room and the time. *Getting more information wasn't a commitment, right?* She would just go and see what it was all about.

That evening, Melanie sat in the back of the room and watched a video about the kids in the orphanage. Everyone was drawn to the cute preschoolers in the video, their chunky cheeks and fresh eyes. They seemed like they could easily be your child, someone you would want to bring in and love. However, Melanie couldn't pull her eyes off of a group of boys who stayed in the background during the whole video. One in particular seemed defiant—arms folded, glaring at the world.

That one! That one! That one! Lord, I hear you!

In that moment, Melanie committed herself to God and to those eyes that in the last ten seconds of the video turned toward the camera, almost daring her to respond. Before the night was over, she had paid for the first three months of sponsorship and was holding his packet, with his picture and his story, in her arms.

Adrian. Well now, there's a name for the assignment I have been itching for. Adrian, you have no idea, but I am coming for you. Backed by an army of angels, I am coming.

Adrian was dangerously close to despair. School felt like a daily battleground. He mostly held it together while he was with his peers, but at the orphanage he lashed out at his dorm brothers and his encargada. This boy who had once been so positive and strong was falling deeper and deeper into a hole of anger and depression. Everything about him shouted it—his stormy expression and the way he carried himself revealed a boy who was angry at the world and disappointed in himself.

"Everyone gather in the *comedor* in fifteen minutes! It's time to write our sponsors." Adrian heard the announcement at the end of dinner and wanted to hide. Both of his brothers had sponsors (they were younger and cuter in every picture taken). He imagined there was a long line of people who wanted to be in their lives, but not his. He was eleven, and not so cute anymore. These days he found it difficult to smile at all, much less for the orphanage pictures.

From Beth's Journal

If I imagine this piece of paper, the one I'm writing on right now, is the heart of an orphan, I have to realize how many times it has been ripped in two. With every disappointment, every hurt, every struggle, from the first time they were abandoned, to the birthday parties they never got, to the many lies they have been told, their hearts are torn again and again and again, until there is nothing but the smallest scrap left. And so we have to love that scrap, and add to it, and keep adding until there is room for the gospel to sit and take hold of their hearts.

The kids without sponsors were supposed to help the others write their letters—a "special" duty. But Adrian knew what was up. It was just a way to try to include everyone. Normally he didn't mind it, walking around and helping the little kids to sound out words and form their letters. But this time he just couldn't face it. He started to head back to his room.

"Adrian, come over here and sit at this table." The office manager directed him through the entrance. "I want to tell you a little about your sponsor so you can write your letter."

Adrian was stunned. *Someone picked me?*

POST CARD

PO NCE

Typical meals in Guatemala are similar to Mexican food. Dishes often include corn, beans, rice, cheese, and tortillas.

Comedor means "dining room."

Writing checks wasn't enough. Melanie wanted to engage Adrian. She was constantly thinking about him, wondering what he was doing, how school was going. The missionary had encouraged sponsors to write to the children they chose. Melanie decided to keep a journal for Adrian. In it she wrote about her dreams for him and recorded her prayers for him each time she said them. She wrote a bit about her own story and her desire to visit him one day.

She sent the journal off, wondering when or even if the boy would read it. She felt like Jesus was reading her heart and hearing her prayers. She just hoped they weren't too late.

Even after he had been told about his sponsor, a woman named Melanie, Adrian couldn't quite believe it. And yet, he felt different. Things didn't automatically go more smoothly and he didn't become immediately happy, but something had entered his life again that had been missing for a while—hope. And not just hope in something that might happen, like a wish that never gets granted, but hope in a person who was real. A living person somewhere out there who actually cared about him. Adrian knew the

workers at the orphanage cared about him too, but he always kind of felt like they had to. But Melanie was someone who was choosing to care about him. He wondered, *Why? Why me?*

When the first journal arrived from Melanie, Adrian took it away to his room and devoured it, slowly taking in each page. He could have had someone read it to him, but he tried to work out the English as best as he could on his own. She sounded so nice! And she asked him questions. He pulled out a pen and started trying to answer them. Even though it was hard to do, it somehow didn't feel like work at all.

Over the next year, the little journal flew back and forth between Guatemala and the U.S., holding in it talk of favorite colors and movies, family stories and sorrows, private questions and dreams. Adrian looked forward to it coming with the same eagerness and excitement as if it were Christmas each time. After a while, he found himself enjoying telling about his own life as much as he liked to read about hers. Things had started to get better at the children's home. His brothers were thriving and becoming more independent, and Adrian no longer felt angry at the world.

Melanie continued to pray for Adrian: for his physical health and his spiritual awakening. She prayed for his schoolwork and his past wounding and his social life. She prayed for him throughout each day, so that even the most mundane tasks took on new meaning. Her mindless drive to work became a time to pray for and think about Adrian's life. The most ordinary office tasks were just part of the way she was earning money that she could give to Adrian, or save for a trip to see him. She was thinking and working for someone other than herself, and she loved it! And all the while, all this focused attention was making her fall more and more in love with a child she had not ever met.

Before she knew it, a year had flown by and it was the morning of her flight. She packed her suitcase carefully, making sure that each of the little presents she was bringing along for Adrian and his brothers would be safe. She prayed, "God, I don't know what you've got in mind for this trip, but I'm up for anything you want me to do."

Adrian went outside, after a dinner he could barely eat, so he could see the car the moment it pulled through the gate. Even though his heart was beating fast, he found himself yawning. He hadn't slept much last night. He kept lying there thinking, *She's coming! She's coming tomorrow!*

He asked his brothers to play somewhere nearby, so he could introduce them immediately to his friend. *Friend? Sponsor? What should I call her?* She meant so much to him, he couldn't think of a word that sounded right. She had done so much for him over the past year. He had thought a lot about what he wanted to say to her. He rolled the English phrases around in his mouth as he stood there, waiting and watching

and practic-
ing. Then
the car
headlights
appeared.

With its volcanoes and jungles, and picturesque villages built on steep hills, Guatemala is a beautiful country.

"She's here! She's here!" he shouted to anyone within earshot.

Panic rose up in his throat. *What if I'm not what she's expecting? What if I can't talk to her?* He pushed the anxious feelings down and swallowed hard. A woman stepped out of the backseat and scanned the play yard. Then her eyes locked onto his.

"Hello, Melanie." Adrian tried to be formal, stepping forward with his hand out, but his shaking voice betrayed him.

"Hola, Adrian!" Melanie tried to seem casual, but her arms reached out. And right there, under the blanket of heavenly hosts, a connection was cemented between two people of different colors, backgrounds, ages, and languages.

God writes the best stories . . . and this one was just beginning.

That visit became the first of many. Melanie came several times a year to guide Adrian through everything from homework assignments to haircuts. She came when he needed some teeth pulled, and she showed up almost overnight when a girl first broke Adrian's heart. She had become for Adrian what he had always dreamt of—someone who was wild about him.

She cared about the small things. Adrian would often jump on the office computer in the orphanage to send Melanie messages about something one of his brothers had done or about the last-minute goal he made at a soccer game. Melanie always sent a message back, sometimes right away, either encouraging him or consoling him, depending on what the occasion required.

But she also cared about the big things. She prayed with him and talked with him about his faith and his future. She asked him important questions about what he wanted to do with his life and she made him think about his behavior.

Melanie laughed and shook her head as she turned from the computer screen back to the lunch she was eating at her desk. Sometimes she couldn't believe it herself—that such an ordinary person like her, who hadn't before even really known exactly where Guatemala was, was now planning her calendar around visits to a Guatemalan orphanage and checking her messages every day to see what Adrian's latest news was.

As Adrian became increasingly important to her, he captured the attention of her whole extended family. They noticed the difference in her life, how she had a passion and inspiration that was on a different level from the way she had lived before. Not long after her first visits to see Adrian, her entire family joined her. And they fell just as passionately for Adrian, calling him more than a friend— they received him as a brother and a son.

Five years later, Adrian shook his head in frustration as the Internet con-nection froze up and Melanie's voice became garbled. Thanks to hundreds of letters and journal pages from Melanie, and a strong desire to talk with her and her family without an interpreter, he was fully bilingual now and often grew annoyed when he was stopped in midstream of conversation by unreliable technology.

Corina, passing by, heard Adrian's sigh and popped her head in. She watched him for a moment as he pushed buttons and shook the mouse, trying to make the computer do what he wanted. She couldn't help but smile at this boy, now a young man of six-teen, and think about how there would have been a time when he might have just hurled the whole machine out the window. But now he was self-controlled and patient. No doubt being part of a beautiful family, parented and guided through the decisions of adolescence with compassion and love— even from another country!—had played a huge role in shaping him into the person sitting there today.

"Can I help you?" Corina asked, her eyes twinkling.

Adrian turned around with a start and then looked sheepishly at her with a contagious smile. "No, it will be OK. I just needed to hear Melanie today. I'm sure it will come back on in a second." Corina nodded and laughed and went on her way, knowing it really would all be OK.

He sat and thought while he waited for the system to reboot. He had been feeling complacent lately, and now he was itching to do something. Something that mattered. He was active in his local church and in the youth group that some of his dorm brothers also attended. He had been involved in some community service projects. These things felt good, but he wanted to do more.

"Adrian, are you there?" He heard Melanie's voice and then her face reappeared on the screen.

"Yes! I'm so glad you're back! Anyway, do you know what I'm talking about? Have you ever felt like that? Like you know God has something more for you,

The Lord makes firm the steps of the one who delights in him.
—Psalm 37:23

but you don't know where to look?"

The corners of her mouth curled up. She looked thoughtful. "I had a season when I was thinking about my own kingdom more than God's. When I was too focused on the world I lived in and not asking enough about the whole world God loves." She leaned in closer to the camera and looked straight at him. "Have you asked him where he wants you to go? Who it is he wants to put you in relationship with? You have a huge story and a huge heart. Ask God! Ask him where he wants you to share your story."

"I will," Adrian said. Melanie promised she would pray for him too, and then said good-bye and signed off. Adrian was still sitting there staring at the blank screen when Corina came back into the office.

"Still not fixed?" she asked.

"No, it's fine. I was just thinking." He got up and started to leave, but then asked, "Corina, you have known me a long time. I want to do something for

God—to give back in some way for all that has been given to me. . . . When you look at me, what do you see? What do you think I could do?"

She sat on the edge of the desk and plunked an armful of files down with a thump. Folding her arms, she studied him for a minute. "Well, I'll tell you what I know. I know you are a boy who spent a long time feeling like you were worth nothing. So that made you develop a love for the underdog, the oppressed, *los indefensos*. You spent a long time taking care of your brothers, and that made you a leader. You had everything taken away from you, but now you have much to offer. With Melanie's encouragement, you've spent a long time writing down the events of your life and so now, you have a story to tell. A story of being led out of fear and hopelessness and neglect into trust and *esperanza* in Jesus and a life of beautiful purpose."

POST CARD

CORRESPONDENCE

Los indefensos means "the helpless."

Esperanza means "hope."

As Corina reflected these truths back to Adrian, an idea began to bubble to the surface. *What about taking the broken and wounded who are part of my family here to reach out to the broken and wounded who are alone? Maybe they could offer something to people who had nothing . . . or just let them know they were seen.*

A few weeks later, he gathered the small group of teenage boys together at his dorm, including his two brothers. "Corina has agreed to take us across the city, around the mountain to the trash dump. Many people are living there who have nothing. Maybe you don't think you have much to give, but we have energy, the ability to work, food, and smiles. And we have our testimonies, about who we are and who our God is—how we are sons of the King. So that's all we need, right? Who's with me?"

Hands shot up around the room.

When they arrived at the dump, Adrian stopped to pray with the young men before they left the van. "God, help us to be ready. To be ready to pray with people with heavy burdens. To be ready to give—and to give more than we have, more than is expected. Help us to be ready to see you move in ways we can't imagine."

They poured out of the van, setting up tables for food and bringing out piñatas. Before long, a hundred people had gathered—scavengers who spent their days looking for food in the dump or for things they could sell for food. Dust swirled and children ran about as the boys from the children's home led songs and played games.

Each in his own way, the boys shared their stories. They told how they too had once just survived from day to day, without hope for anything better. But now they lived fully, because God had given them new life. And even though their hands were not full of all the things money could buy, they had so much to give, because God provided everything they needed.

Tears flowed as stories were exchanged. As the day came to a close, the people formed lines and waited patiently as the boys passed out beans, rice, and the hygiene products they had brought. Adrian

More than 10,000 people live on the Guatemala City dump. A family working twelve hours in a day might be able to make about $3.

walked around, watching the faces of the people in line and praying silently for them. He thought about that dark time when he and his brothers had lived with his parents, and how much they would have loved it if anyone had come to their neighborhood and brought such a party as this. He remembered how much it meant just to be seen, when you felt no one was watching. To know someone out there knew your name, and was calling for you.

A sound behind him made him turn around, and he saw someone, an older man, half hiding behind some rocks. He was very dirty—so dirty Adrian couldn't even really tell how old the man was, but he could see deep lines in his face. Adrian thought he remembered seeing the man sitting there earlier. *Has he been sitting here all day?* Adrian wondered. His eyes traveled down to the man's feet and he realized the man had no shoes. One foot looked like it had a recent wound. Adrian couldn't tell for sure, but it looked infected. *How does he get around this dump with no shoes? How many times has he cut himself? I wonder if he even notices the wounds anymore.*

Adrian watched him for a few minutes, trying not to stare. He remembered a recent picture Melanie had sent him of her whole family, including her grandparents. This man could be someone's grandfather. Someone's father, or brother, or son. He wondered where the man grew up. *Did he know someone in line? Did he know about Jesus?*

Adrian hesitated a moment, not sure what to do. But then he heard the Shepherd calling his name, leading him out, and he followed his voice.

He walked over to the man and sat down near him. He looked down at his shoes. They were nice tennis shoes that Melanie's sponsorship money had supplied for him—shoes he had only recently bought, since his feet seemed to be growing faster than the rest of him. He untied the laces and placed the pair of shoes quietly beside the man. The man's eyes looked scared. "No, no, no," he said, pushing the shoes away. But Adrian knelt down and began to gently put the shoes on the man's feet. As he did, he whispered softly the truths of the gospel message, "You are loved. You are chosen. You are forgiven." And as he said those words and tied the laces, Adrian heard the words as if they were being said to him. He felt years of shame and loneliness and guilt and disappointment melt away.

He stood up and squinted into the setting Guatemalan sun. The man moved to get up, to grab Adrian's hand. But Adrian just clasped his hand and motioned for him to stay in his seat. "These are a gift to you. Not from me, but from the God who saw you here long before I arrived. From the one who knows your name."

Then Adrian turned back toward the rest of the group. The boys were packing up the supplies and loading the van. He smiled at his little brothers, who were hugging children and handing out the last bits of candy. He walked over to them and put his arms around the boys. "Let's go home."

"OK, big brother," Mateo grinned. Adrian ruffled up Felipe's hair and laughed. He looked around at the faces of the people who lived there and smiled and waved good-bye to them. He felt sure he would see them again soon. He knew this was where God wanted him to serve. Adrian couldn't wait to get back to the orphanage and tell Melanie about everything that had happened.

He turned and looked up at the rocks where the older man had been sitting, but he was gone. Adrian smiled and headed off to the van. Barefoot.

REMEMBER THIS

If you think you have nothing to give, ask God to show you what you have, and you might be surprised. In his letter, James advises those who think they lack wisdom to ask God for it—who "gives generously to all without finding fault"—and God will give them what they lack. The wisdom many of us need in order to give is exactly what God shows us. We need to give to all, without finding fault—either in ourselves or in the ones we are giving to. Whether it is time, a hand, money, or even just a few kind words and eye contact, every one of us has the ability to let another human being know they are loved. No matter what.

"Each of you should give what you have decided in your heart to give, not reluctantly or under compulsion, for God loves a cheerful giver. And God is able to bless you abundantly, so that in all things at all times, having all that you need, you will abound in every good work" (2 Corinthians 9:7, 8).

What was given and received in this story? How do you think giving helped Melanie? How do you think giving helped Adrian? How do you think giving helps you? What do you want to give away?

Chapter 3
ANNE-MARIE'S CALL

Esther wrung her hands. There just weren't enough *gourdes* for next month. *Lord! What are you doing? What is your plan? What is it that you want?* She needed air.

The woman walked down the little dirt drive that led up to the house where she had run an orphanage for most of her adult life. When she reached the His Garden Orphanage sign, she leaned against the tree it was on and thought about better times, when the home had been filled with children and she, with the help of many donors, had been able to provide for

POST CARD

CORRESPONDENCE

Haiti shares an island with another nation called the Dominican Republic. Haiti is the poorest country in the Western Hemisphere.

The gourde is Haiti's unit of currency. One U.S. dollar equals about 43 Haitian gourdes.

them. They had had their ups and downs, yes, but nothing as bad as the situation she was in now. If something didn't change soon, she would have to shut the doors. Permanently.

She closed her eyes and lifted her face up to the hot Haitian sun. *Then what will happen to the children?*

Six months later, the funds that had been dwindling were now used up. It had been two years since the great earthquake rocked the island country, and the world had moved on to other disasters and needs. The white vans that used to show up full of help and hope and resources were seen less and less. Haiti was no longer a celebrity cause, and while the needs continued to grow, the hope was fading fast.

Esther had seen this coming. Over the past year, as visitors came and family members made contact, she had informed people that if they could take the children back at all, or knew of someone who could (friends or family), this was the time to do it. Esther had knocked on every door she could

think of, but many people were in the same situation. They had nothing left to give. No food, no money, no room.

But slowly over the next year, kids left for vacation and never returned, as they went to stay in new homes. Esther hated to see their little family break apart, and she prayed regularly for the kids as they came to mind. *Were they eating? in school? with safe people?*

Now the home that started out with thirty kids was down to twenty. *That's ten less mouths to feed and ten less bodies to clothe.* Esther sighed, knowing it wasn't enough. She prayed diligently for the ones left behind. *Who will come for them?*

Derson grew up knowing God had a plan for his life. He didn't always understand it, or even like it, but he felt like there was a holy stamp in his heart, meant for something to come. When he arrived at Tom's house, a place for boys without fathers (or direction), he soaked up the teaching and ministry opportunities. Tom nurtured in him the gifts God had given him. One day, they began to talk about destiny.

"Why do you think all of this happened to me? to my family? Why did God allow it?" Derson asked Tom, while they were out on a gas run.

"I think you are asking the wrong question," Tom replied. "Ask instead: How are you going to use what has happened to you? How will you allow him to use your story line? What will you do with what he has placed in your hands? How will you comfort others in the way you have been comforted?"

Derson shrugged his shoulders and went quiet. He had never thought of it like that before, like he had something more to offer now instead of something less.

They rode in silence for a while.

Finally Derson said, "I guess I could talk to other kids without fathers. Tell them what I have seen God do for me. How I've seen him protect me, provide for me, guide me . . ."

Tom nodded in affirmation. "Maybe God is stirring in your heart someone specific he wants you to reach out to and comfort. Ask him. He will answer."

Christmas came and went on the island and by Easter, there were just twelve children left at His Garden Orphanage. These were the neediest of all; they came from families who never visited.

Esther began again to reach out to extended families of family members, and friends of the families. With any contact she came across, she followed up by asking, "Is there anyone you know who could take in this child?" She called and inquired, begged and encouraged, and occasionally someone would come to the gate. At this point, the child usually didn't recognize the person, and Esther had to spend as much time convincing the child to go with the family member or friend as she had convincing them to come. It was mentally, emotionally, and spiritually exhausting.

The other children watched from their hiding places, waiting to see who would come to the gate, and who would leave this time. By now there was no way to spin the story, all the kids knew what was happening. They were worse than orphans; they were the orphans of orphans.

Derson had more questions than answers, but he remembered Tom's words of encouragement to keep his eyes open and his feet ready, and the rest God would make clear. One afternoon, while walking home from school, he saw a small sign on a tree with an arrow pointing down a dirt road. It read simply, "His Garden Orphanage."

"That's funny. I've never heard of an orphanage around here before and I'm sure I've never even seen this sign," he mentioned to his friend, who was walking home with him.

"You haven't? It's been here in the neighborhood for at least twenty years."

"Let's go and check it out!" Derson said excitedly. "Maybe there are children I can help, right here in my own neighborhood!" His friend smiled at him, hit him on the shoulder, and replied, "That's great. You should go there. I would, but I have to get home and take care of my brother so my mom can go to work. Tell me tomorrow what you find out."

And just like that, Derson was alone. He was wondering if this was what Tom meant about keeping your feet ready. *Ready for what, Lord? Ready to walk into the orphanage and introduce myself and say "I don't have any money. I don't really know how to fix many things, but I do know how to talk about Jesus." No one wants words, they want money, they want action.* Before he knew it, he had talked himself out of going.

You know how to love.

Where did that come from? It was a thought he heard in his mind, but felt in his heart. Then he heard it again.

You know how to love. Just go and leave the rest up to me.

Derson shook his head and hesitated. Then he turned on his heel and walked down the road to His Garden Orphanage.

Summer came to the island, with its unbearable heat. Now there were only six kids left in the home. The staff had dwindled to just Esther, so her time was split between maintaining the home as cook, teacher, laundress, office manager, and house mom, and calling around to see who had any interest in taking the last of the children. Meals were scarce and good news didn't come often.

Anne-Marie was one of the six remaining children. There was another girl, named Kim, and then a set of four brothers. Anne-Marie had been watching and listening to Esther closely in the last few weeks. She could tell Esther was frustrated and didn't know what else to do. When Anne-Marie thought about leaving this home—her home—she felt sad and angry at the same time. So she just tried not to think about it much at all. But now even that was hard to do.

It was clear to everyone at the home that Esther had run out of leads and out of money. It used to be that sometimes, someone would show up at the door with some extra food, but that was happening less and less.

Then one day, in the middle of June, a pastor who had stopped by several times over the years came with a group. He told a story about a family an hour away who was looking for a girl to help them with their younger children. It wasn't the ideal situation, but ideal had stopped being an option long ago. The girl, Kim, left at the day's end to go with this new family.

As Kim was packing up to go, Anne-Marie over-heard Esther talking to the pastor. "It's going to take a miracle for the rest of the children to find a home." Anne-Marie lay down on her mattress alone in the dorm that evening and cried and cried. She cried for all the friends who had left, who she didn't know if she'd ever see again. She cried for a family she didn't know and didn't remember. She cried because she was tired of not being in control. She cried because she was hungry. Finally her gasps slowed down and the tears dried up and she fell asleep, dreaming of the day when someone—anyone—would come for her.

"*Bonjou!*"

Someone was tapping on the gate with a key. Esther could hear it from her room. *Two knocks this week! What are the odds? I wonder who it could be. Maybe one of those leads has panned out.*

Her heart sank when she was greeted at the door by a young man with nothing in his hands.

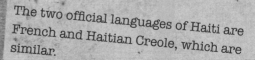

POST CARD

POR   NCE

The two official languages of Haiti are French and Haitian Creole, which are similar.

Bonjou! means "Hello!"

Derson had been practicing what he would say all the way down the road to the orphanage. As soon as Esther opened the door, he took a deep breath and started in, "My name is Derson, and I live at the Lighthouse with Tom." He hesitated. (Everyone knew Tom—right?) The woman at the gate showed no glimmer of recognition, but Derson plowed on. "I have been praying and feeling like God wants to use me more in the life of fatherless children . . ." His voice trailed off and he realized he had run out of things he had planned to say. "I mean, like me. I am fatherless. I want to tell them how God found me." He looked pleadingly at Esther, "Can I come in?"

Esther looked dubious. Derson could tell she was sizing him up. No money. No food. No supplies. Derson started feeling extremely self-conscious. Thankfully, at that moment, the littlest of the four brothers came running around the corner, being chased by one of the older ones. Derson scooped him up just in time for him to avoid a stick to the leg. "Hold on there, little man! Where are you going so fast?"

The woman watched him as he played with the boys and talked with them. Derson had always had an easy time getting children to warm up to him.

"Well," the tired woman said, "I'm Esther, and these are four very active little boys. I am tired of refereeing them. If you could stay for about an hour, you could watch them while I try to make some dinner."

Derson nodded. He couldn't even find the words to say; he was just thrilled to be able to help. Less than fifteen minutes ago, he'd just been on his way home from a normal school day. Now here he was, taking a step toward what he thought God's plan was for him.

The hour passed quickly. Derson played basketball with the boys and by the time dinner was ready, they were hanging all over him, asking when he would come back. Derson promised to be back as soon as he could, but told the boys that in the meantime, they could feel safe knowing God sees them and cares for them. He prayed briefly with them before he walked out the gate.

The whole while Derson was playing with the boys, Anne-Marie had been watching from her balcony.

Does God really see me? Anne-Marie couldn't believe it. *No!*

The four brothers weren't her favorite playmates and she wouldn't even call them her brothers, but still, there was a bond. They were orphans in this home together, and had shared meals, experiences, and a roof for as many years as they could remember. So when an uncle finally came forward to pick up the boys, Anne-Marie felt sick to her stomach.

It's not fair! She silently screamed inside as she helped the boys gather their few belongings. As they walked out the gate with their uncle, Anne-Marie couldn't even look at them. She didn't want to see them looking back at her, with eyes full of pity.

No one wants to be last.

Esther put her arm around Anne-Marie's nine-year-old shoulders and squeezed. A tiny feather of hope floated into Anne-Marie's mind. *Well, since everyone else is gone, maybe Esther will let me live with her forever.*

But at the same time, Esther was thinking, *Only one more to go, and then I can leave for the DR and finally finish my studies.*

Anne-Marie wanted to talk with Esther about staying with her. There were all kinds of promises she was ready to make: *I will be good; I won't eat too much; I will do well in school; I will help you . . .* But she just wasn't sure how to start that conversation. She tried moving into Esther's room later that day. But Esther encouraged her to stay where she was.

Confused and hurt, Anne-Marie went to climb her favorite tree. She hoped no one would see her up there. She just wanted to disappear.

Derson walked up to the gate, happy to get to spend some time with the kids again. But as he got close to the building, a voice seemed to float down from the sky. This time he was sure it was not the voice of God. It sounded very much like a little girl.

"The brothers were picked up an hour ago by an uncle. And I don't know where Esther is. So you might as well just turn around and go too."

Derson cocked his head to the side and looked up through the branches at the angry little girl. "Have I seen you before? I don't remember you from the other day. Are you new?"

"New!?" Anne-Marie half-laughed, half-spit the word out. "No, I am not new. I'm old. That's why no one wants me. I've been around for a long time and I will be for a long time more. What about you? Are you new?"

Derson ignored her mocking tone and replied, "Well, I guess I am a bit new. I just came over to see if any children would like to play." Derson looked at her and then around the yard.

"There aren't children around anymore," Anne-Marie replied. "There is just me. Only me." Her voice dropped a bit. "But . . . we could play on that swing over there, if you could fix it."

Derson smiled. "Let's see what we can do."

Anne-Marie had a wonderful afternoon with Derson. Although he was a lot older, he was fun to play with, like a big brother. Before he left, he reminded her that God loved her. "And sees me, too!" she blurted out.

"Yes!" he grinned. "Were you listening the other day when I was talking to the boys?"

Though she never would have admitted it before, now she happily shook her head. "Yes, I was hiding and watching you all play. I am glad you came back. Please come again!"

Derson prayed in his heart as he replied. "I hope to. I am asking the same God you are for direction, protection, and provision. As he answers, I will go. Let's both listen for him."

After watching Derson leave, Anne-Marie set off to find Esther to tell her all about how her day had gotten so much better. As she hopped from stone to stone in the yard, she remembered truths Derson had spoken to her. *God loves me. God sees me. God has a path for me. God leads me. God speaks to me.*

Her thoughts were shattered when she came up to Esther's office. She didn't mean to eavesdrop, but the door was open and unfortunately, Anne-Marie could hear Esther clearly. "Yes, I am hoping to be able to travel by August. I would like Anne-Marie to be settled somewhere for school before I come to the Dominican Republic."

There were some "hmms" and "ahhs" as Esther listened to the person on the other line. Then she sighed heavily and said, "I've tried everywhere, but no one wants her. She's a great girl, but there isn't anyone out there who cares about that. Then again,

According to UNICEF, there were 380,000 orphans in Haiti before the earthquake. Afterwards, reports say that number doubled.

I can't believe someone came and got those boys. Maybe there's still hope for her yet."

No one wants her.

No one cares.

Maybe there's still hope.

Maybe.

Anne-Marie quickly buried her face in her hands and turned away before Esther could hear the sobs that were rising up in her chest. *No one wants you. No one cares. No one . . .* With each step those words seemed to burn into her eardrums. Those thoughts were hard to take captive. They rolled round and round in her head until she thought she might explode. She threw herself on her bed and sobbed deeply into a blanket.

When this fresh disappointment had grown a little less sharp, Anne-Marie tried to encourage herself. She tried to remember the words Derson had said to her. And she tried hard to believe that a miracle, like Esther had told the pastor, could still happen for her.

*But how, God? Where am I supposed to go? What is
your plan for me?*

When Derson stopped by the next time, about
a week had passed. He had brought with him some
leftover dinner from the Lighthouse meal that night.
"Anyone hungry?" he called through the gate. The
shadows were long and all was quiet.

Anne-Marie barely looked up when she heard his
voice. She had been troubled all week by the call she
had overheard. She waved Derson over to where she
was sitting at the picnic table.

"Hey kid, what's going on? You look like you've
been crying."

Anne-Marie just groaned and buried her head in
her crossed arms.

Derson waited a moment, then nudged her
some more. "Come on. Look up. I felt like God was
nudging me to come here tonight and share some
spaghetti with you. But I don't think he sent me here
just to bring you some spaghetti, OK? So spill it. Why
have you been crying?"

Anne-Marie wiped her face with the back of her sleeve and shrugged. "It's just me. No one wants me. Everyone else—someone came for them. But not for me. Not one relative. Not one pastor. Not one family friend. And I know Esther has tried. I can hear her from her office." She imitated Esther's voice: "Anne-Marie is a generous girl with a sensitive heart. She would be no trouble at all . . ."

I will not leave you as orphans. I will come to you.

—John 14:18

The tears started streaming again down the little girl's face. "No one. NO one. No one wants me." She hid her face in her arms again, embarrassed by her emotion. But she couldn't help it. She had been so lonely, and Derson was the only person she could talk to.

Not knowing exactly what to say or do, Derson dedicated the rest of the evening to lifting his little friend's spirit. He told her silly stories about life in the Lighthouse. He taught her fun songs he had learned at church. He told her all three jokes he knew and adventure stories that were mostly true . . . maybe. He also asked her about what she knew about her family and about the kids who she had played with before they all left.

The sun was almost gone and Derson had to leave to get home before it was completely dark. He left the dinner with Anne-Marie and squeezed her hand, saying, "Remember, God sees you. And he will lead you out."

From Beth's Journal

Oh, Lord, it's always like this, isn't it? Impossible situations, broken people, then the opportunity to step into your story. I don't know what you have in mind, but my answer is always yes. Yes to supporting Derson as he listens to you. Yes to providing a family for this girl. Yes to knowing who, before I know where, how, or when.

Knock, knock.

Uh-oh, what now? Tom thought, though he was certainly used to answering knocks on his door in the night. As the director of a home mostly filled with abandoned boys, he knew that not a day would ever go by when someone wasn't experiencing some kind of minor or major crisis, at least once in the day. He just wished they could all happen in the day and not when he was about to shut his eyes. *Oh well. All in God's time, not mine.* "Yes? Come in."

"I know you are getting ready to sleep, but I need your help. I don't know what I can do, but I think we need to do something." Derson blurted out. He had been seeing Anne-Marie's troubled eyes looking at him all night, even when his own eyes were shut. He just had to talk to someone about it.

"Do what, about whom?" Tom asked, sitting up.

Derson took a deep breath and launched into his story about feeling led to His Garden Orphanage and meeting the kids there, and how they all had to leave. "It's all coming down to this one girl."

"Ohhh," Tom said, rolling his eyes. "It's always a girl."

"No, it's not like that. She's little. She just needs a family. And . . ." he spread his arms out and waved them around, "we are that. We are a family. And she doesn't have anyone else." Derson sat and waited for Tom to

respond to the question he hadn't voiced yet. And Tom
sat and waited for Derson to say it. Finally, Derson said,
"OK, fine. I'll say it. What if we just brought her here?"

Tom stared at Derson and squinted his eyes, cocking
his head and pausing too long for Derson's comfort.
Derson felt like he was holding his breath.

"Let's go. Let's go get her."

"Really?" Derson practically squealed. "Are you
sure?"

"Yes, I'm sure. Welcome to this adventure we call
following God's voice."

The next day, Tom told the group of his plan to
pick up Anne-Marie in the afternoon so she could
settle in before all the kids arrived back from school.
But the Lighthouse kids had other plans. Derson's
enthusiasm had spread to them all, and they all
wanted to meet Anne-Marie.

"Can you wait until we are back from school? So
we can all go and get her?" one of the boys shouted
out.

"Oh yeah! Can we come?"

"Tom, can you take all of us? Please?"

Tom gives instructions to his boys before they head out.

A chorus of voices rang from around the room and Tom looked at Derson, who sat speechless. He looked at all the faces of his brothers and sisters, bound together not by blood, nor by family history, but by this common experience of feeling found after a lifetime of being lost.

Derson nodded at Tom and answered for them both. "Yes. Let's all go and lead her home."

After school, Tom piled them all in the *tap-tap* and they traveled the short distance to His Garden Orphanage. He was surprised by how run-down it had become since his last visit. Esther came out to meet them when she heard the ruckus at the gate.

"Tom!" she exclaimed, and they hugged. An understanding passed between them—the challenge of raising children in this country, at this time, was a call so few had responded to. They exchanged some words and Tom shared with her what was happening with Derson. He thanked her for allowing him to serve there and then went on to say why they had come.

Esther was dumbfounded. She had never imagined God answering her prayers like this. She and Tom talked a few minutes more about the logistics and then turned to the crowd of kids he had brought with him. They had been waiting, but were getting impatient.

He smiled. "It has all been worked out. It's all good." They giggled nervously. Then Tom turned toward the yard and said loudly, "We've come for Anne-Marie." Derson stepped over to the tree he knew was her favorite hideout and motioned for Tom to say it again. "We've come for Anne-Marie!" his voice

POST CARD

CORRESPONDENCE

A tap-tap is what Haitians call a kind of pickup truck with seats and a hood, used for public transportation.

bellowed. He chuckled a little and said to Esther, with a wink, "Esther, is she here?"

"I am HERE!" And at that moment, Anne-Marie did not care how she might appear in front of this group of strangers. Someone wanted her! Someone came to the gate for her! She ran to Derson and hugged his waist. "You came for me!" Tears were pouring down her cheeks.

"No. Jesus came for you. I am just following his lead." Derson led her over to the crowd of children who were watching on tiptoe and climbing up the side of the vehicle to see what was happening. Each one was reminded of the time they first came to the Lighthouse and were welcomed into this mixed-up family. Derson introduced her to the boys and girls. Although shy at first, Anne-Marie soon began to laugh and talk easily with the others. Tom gave her a hug and a certificate the kids had made for her: an official invitation to join their ragtag collection of once-lost children, now found. She hugged it to her heart and looked up at him with a grateful smile. Tom squeezed her shoulders and whispered into her ear just one of the many promises God has for her. When he pulled back, he saw what kept him and others like him going—the face of a child Jesus has moved heaven and earth to find.

How would you feel if you were Anne-Marie, and you were the last orphan left at the orphanage? Has there ever been a time when you felt like you were alone? What did you do?

Psalm 23 talks about the Lord being our Shepherd. "Even though I walk through the darkest valley, I will fear no evil, for you are with me, your rod and your staff, they comfort me" (v. 4). What does it mean to you to know that God will always be with you? Write your thoughts here.

Chapter 4
STEVE'S HOME

Rosemary rubbed her belly. The waiting room was full of people and the air was stuffy and hot. She was tired. Tired of being here, tired of these people, tired of doctors, and tired of life in general. *I suppose that's just as well,* she thought, *since I won't be around much longer.* In her irritation she shouted out to the crowd, "What future do these babies possibly have ahead of them? I won't be around to see it, that's for sure." She laughed bitterly. "That's what HIV does, it takes your future from you. And not just yours, but your babies' too." Heads nodded all around her. Some people stared, some just turned away, not wanting to hear what this woman had to say. But all of them were in the same boat—pregnant and sick, all of them HIV-positive. Rosemary's head fell on her chest. In a room full of women who should have been buzzing with life, you could smell death in the air.

Rosemary's twin boys came in late spring, kicking and screaming into this world, joining their older

brother and two sisters. Together they all lived in a hut with a dirt floor, a typical home for the rural area of Kenya where they lived. It was crowded with the arrival of the new babies, but everyone adjusted. Rosemary left as soon as she could, knowing her days were numbered. The idea that her babies might die soon too was more than she could handle.

Grandma took over as the primary caregiver, but there wasn't much caring in her giving. She was an angry woman who didn't want to assume responsibility for her daughter's mistakes. And that was exactly what she thought of those boys, Steve and Samuel— they were just one big mistake.

Steve didn't even know why one day his brother was beside him and the next day he wasn't. He was too little to understand, and no one tried to explain it to him anyway. It would be years before he realized Samuel was born with the same disease his mother had.

The disease took both of them before he had a chance to know them.

All he remembered of the next stretch of his life was a blur of different homes, different faces, different families. His grandmother tired of the burden of taking care of a baby soon after the deaths of Steve's mother and brother. She made it known in the village that she was looking for a home for the baby boy. A friend of Rosemary's came forward and decided to take Steve in for a while. His grandmother handed over the boy, who was now a toddler. "It's just too much for me to do at my age," she grumbled.

As long as Steve played quietly and no one noticed him, the new house seemed nice. Even though he was very little, he understood that when

he got in the way, the mood in the house shifted. There was stress and fighting and worried faces. He wondered later what it was that made them give him away. *Did I eat too much? Did I talk too much? Maybe I didn't help enough.*

Another friend of his mother stepped in. That was house number 3. Then another friend of a friend after that—house number 4. Steve went on like this for years, bouncing from house to house, never having a place of his own, never fitting in, never belonging, and never knowing why. He lost count of how many homes he stayed in as a child. Dozens? Twenty? Who knows?

Sometimes the family ran out of space. Sometimes they ran out of food or money. Sometimes maybe they just didn't like him. No one ever bothered to explain things to him, so Steve gleaned what information he could from bits of conversations. In the last house he had stayed in, he could remember hearing the mother argue with the oldest son.

"We can't just turn him out. He has no one. Don't be cruel. *Tafadhali*!" the mother pleaded.

"Well, then, *you* go to work. *You* find extra food.

I am not killing myself any longer for someone else's child. Every time we sit down to eat, we have to divide the meal by one more mouth. And what does he do to help? I don't see anything."

Steve longed to jump into the conversation, to defend himself, to plead with the mother, but he already knew how this would end. He had heard versions of this conversation ten times before. He quietly packed his bag, never even said good-bye, and walked out of that village. He had decided to go find his grandmother.

He was thirteen years old.

POST CARD

PO NCE

Swahili is one of the official languages of Kenya. It is the most widely spoken African language, with over 50 million speakers.

Tafadhali means "please."

Brad looked out the window of the friend's house where he had come to have breakfast. The house was close to the airport, and he watched the planes climbing into the sky and flying in low overhead. As he sipped his coffee, he counted the hours before he would be leaving in one of those planes—just 58 hours, 37 minutes, and however many seconds.

Then he had to laugh at himself. No one counted the minutes in Kenya. The people there seemed to live on a completely different system of time. That's one of the reasons he loved it there. No rush. No anxiety about being late to something. Just taking each day as it comes.

His friend returned carrying a plate full of eggs and bacon and hash browns and a waffle. It all looked wonderful. As Brad closed his eyes to pray, he felt especially grateful. He thanked God silently for blessing him with the opportunity to go back to Kenya and help people there—people who had nowhere to call home. Then he opened his eyes and started digging in. It was a huge breakfast—much larger than he would normally eat. But he decided to just enjoy it. His friend had worked hard to make everything nice for him, and besides, he wouldn't be eating breakfasts like this where he was going in Kenya. It was hard to eat like that when people were starving all around you.

After going back to the last place he knew she had lived and asking around, Steve finally found his grandmother, six weeks later.

"Steve, is that you?" she squinted her eyes and cocked her head, as the adolescent version of that toddler she remembered came walking towards her.

Not exactly a warm homecoming, but it was nice at least to be known after some weeks on the street. "Yes, it's me. *Habari*! I have been looking for you everywhere! How have you been? Are you alone? Where are the others?"

"They are in Nairobi together. We all thought you were dead." She said those words as if she was talking about the weather. No look of concern. No apologies. She studied him for a moment without words, then said, "You look like Rosemary now, don't you?"

POST CARD

PONDENCE

Habari is a typical greeting that means "Hello" or "Hello, how are you?"

Riding on a matatu down a Kenyan road.

Steve couldn't have known. He didn't remember his mother, and he had never seen her picture. This was one of a very few times his grandmother had ever even mentioned her. He wasn't sure from the older woman's tone if the resemblance was a good thing or not.

He felt shy under her stony gaze, but he asked, "I was hoping we could go to my brother and sisters? I don't remember much about them, but I am ready to be with family, if you'll have me."

She just nodded and turned back to go into her hut. The matter seemed settled. Steve helped her gather some of her things, then they closed up the hut. Later that same day they boarded a *matatu* and headed for Nairobi. Steve eagerly watched the scenery change outside his window. He couldn't wait to see his family.

"Habari."

"Habari."

The sisters exchanged a look, waiting for their oldest brother, Simon, to speak. They all stared for a moment at each other. To Steve, it felt like an eternity. He knew it would be awkward, coming here, but he still had hoped he would be welcomed into the family. Yet for his siblings, it was as if a ghost was standing before them. A ghost they didn't want to see or think about. To them, Steve was the baby that stole their

POST CARD

CORRESPONDENCE

A matatu is a privately owned minibus or van used for transportation, similar to a taxi.

More than 12 percent of Kenya's children die before the age of five. Causes of death are usually malnutrition, malaria, dysentery, or HIV/AIDS.

mother from them. They had assumed he had died too—so many babies did. They didn't know how to adjust to the stark reality that they had a brother and now here he was, looking familiar and strange all at the same time.

It was Steve who finally broke the silence. "Do you have room for me?"

His question hung in the air for a moment, as everyone waited for Simon to respond. But Simon just nodded at his sister Mercy and walked back inside the shanty home, a structure consisting of metal sheets and wattle, held together with mud.

Mercy replied, "For the moment. That's all we can say. We never know around here how long we'll be able to stay in a place. But for now, go ahead. Come in." The threat of eviction in the city slums put many people in constant fear of having their homes destroyed.

Steve let out a deep sigh. Tonight, in this strange city, he had a roof. This one small room had no electricity, no running water, and no sanitation. Their home was located in the largest shantytown in Nairobi, called Kibera. Like the vast majority of Kibera residents, Steve's family had no toilet. When they could, they would sneak and use a nearby outhouse that belonged to someone else. But at times even that option was prevented by a lock and chain on the door. All through the slums, human waste leached into the water people drank and contaminated the food they ate. Typhoid and other diseases were spread this way, sometimes resulting in deaths (especially young children).

City slum life was very different from what Steve had experienced in the rural village. But to a thirteen-year-old boy, it seemed like an exciting adventure.

Mercy prepared a meal of *ugali* for the family that night. Steve tried to stay out of the way

The situation in the capital city of Nairobi is typical of the challenges facing poor people throughout Kenya's urban areas. Demand for land means that over half of Nairobi's population is crammed into just 1.5 percent of the total land area.

in a corner of the room. It was nice to be with family, yet he felt odd. He didn't know what to do—he had never been in his own home, and he didn't even remember what it was like to live with brothers and sisters. The conversation that evening was somewhat strained, but no one was fighting. As Steve curled up on a mat in his corner and drifted off to sleep, he felt hopeful.

Within weeks, however, it was clear that the family already had a system for living and working together. And that system didn't include Steve. Knowing he had a better chance on the streets than his Grandma did, one morning when he left to go out and look for things to sell, he just decided not to come back.

No one came looking for him.

POST CARD

CORRESPONDENCE

Typical meals in Kenya are filling and inexpensive. Staple foods are corn, maize, beans, and potatoes.

Ugali is a thick kind of cornmeal porridge.

Over the next three years, Steve made what living he could on the streets. Every now and then he would return to his family, and Grandma would take him back sometimes. But within days her mistreatment of him would get so bad, Steve would leave (or be kicked out). Life was definitely not any easier on the streets, but at least it wasn't so hurtful.

Street kids do whatever it takes to get through the day. They steal, cheat each other, and sell—trading whatever they have for a meal, or a roof, or a book. Steve spent his days sorting through garbage, looking for things to recycle, but there wasn't always a profit at the end of the day and he had to eat. He sank to new lows in his life, doing things he'd never imagined, just to stay alive.

A shantytown in Kenya.

Brad had been working in the camps for internally displaced persons for a few months before he made his first visit into town. The camps were filled with people who had been driven out of their homes due to political unrest and violence that had happened in their country. Aid workers did what they could to help, but thousands of people still were suffering from poor housing, malnutrition, and little access to the health services they needed. Some days taking care of these people seemed like a hopeless job that would never end, but other days Brad was encouraged by the number of people he talked to who still had faith—they knew the God they followed had a better plan for them. It was one they couldn't see now, but they trusted God to lead them through this dark valley and into a brighter chapter.

In town Brad was struck by simple pleasures: the structure of town life, the friendly banter in the marketplace, people hanging out freshly washed clothes to dry. But he was also saddened to see so many kids on the streets—no one to care for them or protect them. No place to call home. He wondered, *Where do they all come from? How do they get by?* And more and more, he found himself hearing a voice speaking inside of him, *What are you going to do about it?*

Steve had tried to stay in school, doing so more often than not—enough to get to the equivalent of seventh grade by the time he was fifteen.

"Steve, I see in you potential, a softness underneath your hard shell. Why are you here in my office again?" The director of the school spoke to him with authority after Steve had been sent there for fighting in class. "I appreciate the challenges you face in getting here every day, but once you are here, you need to see yourself as a student, and not as a street kid. Those instincts have served you well outside, but now, in the classroom, you have to work together, with your classmates. Who do you want to be in school? What do you see yourself as right now?"

Right now? Steve thought, *Well, right now I see myself as cornered, trapped. And I don't like trapped. This week alone, I have had an injury from jumping a fence while stealing some bread; I made another enemy on the street, which is making sleep hard to come by; and I failed a test I thought I didn't need to worry about. I haven't seen my family in over a year and now, at school, the only place I can relax, I keep getting into trouble when I try to defend myself. And the threat of school ending is coming, and I don't know what I'll do after that. That's how I feel.*

But instead of all of that, he answered, "I see myself as running out of options."

The director went on to say many things, but Steve tuned him out. He knew he didn't have any real choice in the matter. He could sit quietly and listen and hope they let a failing troublemaker stay another day in school, or he could fight back and be aggressive and never see the inside of another classroom. So he stayed silent and looked agreeable.

Later that day, after school was finished, Steve found himself walking the streets of Nairobi. He didn't have any idea where he was going, right now, or in the future. He was out of money, out of ideas, and all out of hope. He kicked at a pile of

Street boys in Kenya.

trash and cried out, "God help me! If you are real, I need help."

For most poor children in Kenya, school is not a possibility. For those who do get to go, only 1 in 10 will complete eighth grade.

And though in this moment Steve felt very alone, the truth was there were many just like him, kids wandering the streets, with no one checking in on them. These children formed their own versions of families, and Steve was part of one of these groups.

Shortly after Steve cried out for help, several of his street friends saw a sign that advertised a safe place to sleep at night. It was a church nearby.

The first thing Steve noticed about the church was the smell, or rather, the lack of it. Anyone who took more than a couple steps into Kibera was hit by the stench of the green-brown waste water flowing in open ditches. The foul river carried not just sewage, but also chemicals from farming estates outside

Others, like seed sown on good soil, hear the word, accept it, and produce a crop—some thirty, some sixty, some a hundred times what was sown.

—Mark 4:20

the slum. It was littered with garbage, plastic bags, and glass bottles all along its path. But the church was clean and the air smelled fresh. There were no piles of litter or puddles of sewage here. Steve barely remembered what it was like to live in a fresh, clean space.

For a year, Steve and his friends spent their nights in the church shelter, making it to class most days, and eating at least one meal each day together at the church.

While their bodies were fed and cared for, their minds were given some things to work on as well. There they heard about Jesus, and how he loved them. They heard about grace and forgiveness and about becoming something new. But these young hearts had been hurt enough and deceived enough in their short lives that none of the boys was willing to trust anyone—especially not a God they couldn't see. No one in the church shelter pushed them, so while they lived and listened and learned, seeds were planted in their hearts, but never took root.

Steve was eating dinner with his friends one night when he realized he was feeling at peace for the first time in a long time. Things had been going well at school, he was learning to control his emotions, and the safety and consistency of this church-home in his life set him free from the stress of always looking for another meal or another spot to lay his head at night.

All these good feelings had allowed Steve to dream a bit about being with his family again. So that night as they were eating, he announced, "Hey *marafiki*, I have been thinking about going back to see if my family will take me in. I'm older now; I can help them out, you know? Not just be one more person to divide the food between. What do you think? Think they would let me in? Have you all ever thought of returning to your families?"

POST CARD

Marafiki means "friends."

Everyone started talking at once, encouraging Steve, and talking about their own families. That night he went to bed with a settled heart. He was going to go home.

He had always known where they were. He was pretty sure they were in the same shanty he'd left them in. Finding them had never been the issue.

When he walked up to the doorway, his grandmother came out. She squinted up into the sun and looked hard at him, making sure she knew him. Then she pointed back the way he had come and barked, "Go back! Get away! There's nothing for you here!"

Steve stepped back, more stunned than if she had hit him. He looked one long, last time at her, and then ran away. Past the entrance to the slum, past the first place he stole something, past his school, and eventually past the church. He couldn't stop. He didn't want to stop.

As his feet pounded on the dirt road, the words pounded in his head. *You are worthless. No one wants you. What would your mother think of you if she had lived? What kind of son isn't even wanted by his own family?* He could not turn around. He could

never go
back there.
He had no
family to
return to, only
shame.

Steve ran
and ran until
he couldn't
move his legs
anymore. He
rested alongside
the road in some
bushes. Then he started running again. He decided
to run until the smell and the lights of Nairobi were
far behind him. By midnight, he had come to a town.
The sign beside the road said, "Welcome to Kijabe,
Place of the Wind." Kijabe was twenty-five miles from
Nairobi.

Perfect, he thought, *that's how I feel, like a cloud
of dust, blown by the wind*.

Kijabe is a small town in the heart of the Rift
Valley and was far more beautiful to Steve than the

busy, crowded, modern city of Nairobi. Steve might have been blown there by the wind, but he was more comfortable in this rural town than anywhere he could remember before.

He knew of this area. There were IDP camps nearby—for internally displaced persons; everyone knew about them. A few years ago, conflict and violence had erupted throughout Kenya, and that, combined with scarce resources and natural disasters, had driven hundreds of thousands of people out of their homes. From what Steve had heard, these IDPs had it as bad as him, and he was curious to see how they lived.

But first, he had to get settled. For Steve, this meant picking through garbage and sorting out recyclable materials. He sold the bits he found to buy enough to make his first *chakula* there, a small pot of ugali and some pieces of a half-rotten potato he had found (he cut off the rotten parts).

Through that first chakula, he also made his first Kijabe friend. Muagi had been on the streets as long as Steve. At first, when Steve asked if he could share Muagi's fire, Muagi was reluctant. He'd never seen Steve around here before, and he wasn't sure he could be trusted. But Steve quickly offered to share half the meal, and that made all the difference.

They provided good company for each other, though as always with street kids, there was a certain level of wariness. Muagi showed Steve warm places to sleep (usually under the farm trucks that parked for the night, heated by the engines that had been working so hard all day long).

A few days after they met, Muagi took Steve out to the camps and introduced him to a whole community of people. Steve listened to their stories with a troubled heart. He had no solutions to offer them. When he told them he had come from Nairobi, people asked

POST CARD

CORRESPONDENCE

Chakula means "meal."

about relatives and friends. *Do you know him? Have you ever seen this woman?* But he didn't know anyone there besides the church workers and his street friends. Steve realized he had never really paid attention to the people he stole or begged from. He had always felt too ashamed to look anyone in the face.

But even though he didn't have the answers they were wanting, Steve felt comfortable with the people in the camps. He could identify with them—feeling like your life wasn't your own, like other people's choices had put you in a place you now couldn't get out of. And through taking the time to listen to them, he felt he was helping them in some small way.

Steve himself felt like all these questions were going unanswered, and that his own cries for help had gone nowhere. But Jesus had heard Steve's cry for help all those months ago in Nairobi. And here in Kijabe, as Steve's heart opened up to other people and he learned to listen, the time came for Jesus to introduce himself.

Brad had just come back from serving at the camps that day and decided to pick up something at the market for dinner. He had a lot on his mind, and he was hoping to have an uneventful night. But as he walked among the stalls he found himself asking God for guidance. He had been frustrated by his efforts to connect with the people in the camps lately. So he asked, *God, help me know who to speak to. Help me know who to sit down with, who needs my attention. I promise I will follow you wherever you send me.*

As Brad came up to a fruit stand, he noticed a teenager sitting alone on the ground with his back propped up against a crate, eating some plantains.

Brad felt a prick in his heart when he looked at him. He prayed for a moment, asking God again for guidance, and he felt urged to go and talk with the young man.

Brad came over and stooped down beside the stranger, who sat up and stiffened at his approach. But Brad had talked to street kids before, and knew not to take their defensiveness personally.

"Habari. My name is Brad. I've been living here in Kijabe for a while now, but I don't remember seeing you around. What's your name?"

"I'm Steve. I only came here a little while ago . . . from Nairobi," Steve offered cautiously.

Brad talked to Steve for a while, explaining why he was there in Kijabe, and telling a little about his work in the camps. Then gently and confidently Brad told Steve about Jesus. He told him that the love of Jesus is what had brought him to Kenya, how he trusted Jesus with his life, and how he wanted to show Jesus' love to others. He told him about how Jesus sees us even when we feel all alone and how he is always with us.

As Brad kept talking, Steve's mind was reeling. He rememberd the words that the church workers in Nairobi had spoken to him about God's love and forgiveness. He heard Brad talking about a God who loves us so much and never stops pursuing us. Steve wondered, *Who was this God and why won't he leave me alone?*

Steve found himself telling Brad his own story.

From street kid to mentor. Steve wants to help boys like him to find a place to belong.

And as Brad listened to him, Steve felt his own heart opening up. This foreigner, this stranger from America seemed to actually care about what he had to say. More than that, he seemed to care about him.

Finally, Brad stood up and offered his hand to Steve. He took it and Brad pulled him up. He said, "So Steve, I've heard about what you've done and where you've been. But what is it you want to do now?"

The answer popped out before Steve could even think about it. "I want to help street boys like me. I want to show them love and give them a home—a family."

Brad knew God was asking him to do more than just listen on that day. When he heard Steve say his dream was to take in street boys like himself, he knew he had to respond.

From that day, Brad and Steve's story lines became woven together, as Brad taught Steve about the author of love, and where a real sense of belonging could be found.

As time went by, Steve's eyes were opened. He began to see boys like himself everywhere he went. And instead of seeing them as potential rivals or pitying them, he began to see them as friends and brothers. He began to see them as Jesus saw them. As Jesus saw *him*.

Together with Brad's help, Steve dreamed and planned for a home for street boys.

Brad was walking along the streets of Kijabe one day when he saw a sickly, fourteen-year-old boy. The boy had been physically assaulted and was bleeding. He was alive, but lying on the ground and not moving.

Brad breathed a quick prayer and approached the boy. "Habari. What's your name?"

"Ken." He answered, breathing hard.

"Ken, my name is Brad. What happened to you?"

"What do you care?" Ken's voice was weak, but hostile.

"I care because Jesus does. He led me over here to you. He sees you. Who did this to you?"

Ken struggled to keep his composure. "I was just trying to get what I deserved. You wouldn't understand." He shrugged and started struggling to get to his feet.

Brad put his hand on Ken's shoulder and asked, "Can I take you to your family? Can I help you get home?"

"I have no family. My mom died when I was young. No one else cares."

Brad hesitated and closed his eyes, pleading with God to lead. When he opened his eyes, Ken was staring at him angrily.

Finally Brad spoke with authority and kindness. "Well, I have a story for you. I was walking through the market here one day when I met a man very much like you . . ."

Steve jumped up when he heard the knock. He was so proud to be living in his own home, he was always glad to have visitors. He swung open the door and grinned widely at his friend Brad.

"Habari! I wasn't expecting you, Brad! And you have brought a new friend?"

"Steve, this is Ken. I've been telling him about you. Ken was in some trouble and needs a safe place to rest. Do you think he could stay with you for a while?"

Ken was the first street kid Steve welcomed into his home. But within two months, Steve and Ken had welcomed in three more.

And that is how the Storyweaver does his work. Steve began forming the family he never had, growing to lean on the Father for provision and wisdom and protection—all the qualities he'd always imagined a dad would offer a family. Ken and the other boys began learning lessons in trust and connection. They watched Steve's actions and listened to what he said about God.

One night at dinner, a new boy named Baraka asked, "Has God really made a difference in your life?"

"Made a difference? Are you kidding me?" Steve said. "I was once lost. So lost. Then he found me. I was just eating my dinner and he found me. Now I am swept up into a story that's about more than just today. I lived a lifetime only wondering about today: What would I eat? What would I steal? Would I go to school? Where would I sleep? Now I know I am a story in the Storyweaver's book, and you all are written into it, too. I thought I was a nobody, with nothing to offer to no one. Jesus changed that. He showed me that the answers to my problems weren't in the hands of my birth family, or of the government, or of anyone in power on this earth."

He looked around the table to see that he had their attention.

"I thought my life was missing everything, but really it was missing only one thing. It was missing Jesus."

He stopped, knowing there was so much more he could say. He wanted so badly for them to understand, but believed in God's perfect timing. He would just be faithful to tell his story, and wait for the Storyweaver to write their chapters. In the meantime, he closed the meal with a prayer, "Jesus watch over our families, wherever they are, direct our steps, and heal our hearts. Amen."

Sometimes it's hard for us to see past our own views. God asks us to go out into the world with his eyes, to see people as he sees, to love as he loves—with unconditional compassion and mercy.

In Jesus' story of the Good Samaritan, we read this (Luke 10:36, 37):

"Which of these three do you think was a neighbor to the man who fell into the hands of robbers?"

The expert in the law replied, "The one who had mercy on him."

Jesus told him, "Go and do likewise."

What does it mean to show mercy to someone? Write your thoughts here.

Chapter 5
SHANNEN'S DREAM

Mama Cony was working in the kitchen. It was a Saturday morning, which meant things got started a little later than usual. The relaxed pace suited her just fine. Most of the children were still sleeping, only a few of them stirred. Dust particles danced in the golden sunlight streaming through the window.

MEXICO

Monterrey

Mexico City

She took another sip of her coffee and looked at her four dozen eggs, assembled there on the counter. It took a lot of eggs to feed so many hungry children. She thanked God for his provision on this day and every day of her life. The words of the Lord came to her, "How often I have longed to gather your children together, as a hen gathers her chicks under her wings, and you were not willing" (Matthew 23:37). She thought of the "chicks" still sleeping in their nests just now and prayed, *Lord, I am willing. Gather us all up under your wings and protect us, Lord.*

Mama Cony

When she opened her eyes, they landed on the cartons of eggs waiting for her. *Well*, she thought, *they aren't going to crack themselves, are they? I had better get started*. And with that, she tied on an apron and began the business of making breakfast for the orphanage.

"Where are we going, Mama?" Shannen asked again, looking up adoringly at her mother. She clipped her little feet along, trying hard to match her mother's swift strides. *Why was she walking so fast?*

Her mother shifted her purse from one shoulder to the other, wondering how many more blocks they had to go. The heat from the Mexican sidewalk was burning through the soles of her cheap shoes. Her feet ached from the long walk and she was weary already, even though it was still early in the morning.

Brushing tears out of her eyes, her mother replied, "Just keep walking and you'll see. We're almost there, it'll be fine. Everything will be fine."

Shannen went back to concentrating on her feet. She made a game of the walking, counting how many steps it took to go between cracks in the sidewalk. *Uno, dos, tres,* there! *Uno, dos, tres, cuatro* . . .

She wondered how many steps they had left to walk. Probably higher than she had learned to count. She was only four years old and had never been to school. But she had a bright, curious mind. That mind was busy right now trying to figure out where they were going. And why didn't her mother let her stop to rest? They had passed bench after bench—she pointed out each one—but her mother seemed bent on getting to wherever it was they were going.

Shannen's mother unfolded the paper in her hand and squinted at the scribbles again. Then she stopped and looked up and turned around, searching for something. Finally, the young woman spotted a street sign and took a sharp right.

After a few more steps, it seemed they had arrived. But where? Shannen looked up at the big house with a tall gate and a sign hanging out in the front. She couldn't tell what the sign said.

Her mother became nervous all of a sudden, pacing back and forth. Thoughts were darting through the woman's mind, the ones that drove her to this place— thoughts she could never hope to explain to the little girl beside her. *You are all alone. You have no business being a mother. You can't even take care of yourself. She will one day leave you like he did.*

But when she bent down by Shannen and straightened the sweet little dress and smoothed her daughter's hair, she had a smile on her face. She picked up the little girl and tapped on the iron gate with a key. Then she put her forehead on Shannen's and whispered again, "*Todo va a estar bien.*"

Mama Cony heard someone tapping against the gate. *At this hour? Visitation isn't until the afternoon!*

Sometimes an occasional guest would come early, but Mama Cony hadn't even finished her first cup of coffee.

C'mon, people.

She walked out of the kitchen, stepping over the toys on the floor and into the shady courtyard where she could see a young mother holding a little girl on her hip. Her heart immediately softened as she realized what she was looking at. *That's what twenty years in this business gives you—insight.* Not to mention compassion, which is what she felt when she looked into that mother's eyes.

"Come on in," Mama Cony's voice was a shock to their ears at first, so deep and raspy. It didn't seem to match her grandmotherly features and kind eyes—eyes that with a look told the real story of the love that filled her up inside. She hugged these two little women, strangers in every sense, and introduced herself. "I was just finishing up some eggs, either of you hungry?"

"Sí!" Shannen blurted out, before her mother could clamp her hand over her mouth. Suddenly they

POST CARD

CORRESPONDENCE

Roughly 90 percent of people living in Mexico speak Spanish as their primary language.

Todo va a estar bien means "Everything will be fine."

were being led into the comedor. Shannen spied a children's kitchen set in the corner of the room and squirmed out of her mother's arms.

Shannen's mother just watched as her child sidled up to another girl already playing there. For a moment, she had forgotten why she came.

Then without warning, she quietly turned to the woman now mixing up eggs, and opened her mouth to speak, "I came here this morning to—"

"I know why you are here, and we'll get to that in a moment." The mother looked a little shocked at this older woman's interruption. But she quickly realized there was no stopping her. So Mama Cony continued, "Only one reason a young woman knocks on the door of an orphanage before 8:00 in the morning. Wanted to do this before you lost your nerve today, eh?" She didn't wait for confirmation, just barreled on, "But first you need to know one thing. In this home, we love Jesus. Do you know Jesus?"

The young woman fidgeted nervously in her seat. Papers to fill out, she had expected. An uncomfortable, humiliating interview, she had prepared for. But questions about Jesus? She wasn't ready for that.

"I will take that as a no. If you knew him, you would shout it from the rooftops. Gather your daughter and let's go in my office. We have some holy business to attend to."

Mama Cony turned her wide figure and shouted to one of the older girls just coming down the stairs, "Gaby, will you serve the eggs this morning? We are going to have church in the office for a little while."

Gaby half-smiled and nodded. Still waking up, she knew it might be a while before Mama Cony returned. When Mama went to have church, you never knew how long it might take. The girl ambled over to the counter to call the children for morning prayer.

With a confident step, Mama Cony moved Shannen and her mother into an office space, where she pulled out a big Bible and opened it like she knew exactly where she was headed.

"Everyone needs *salvación*," she started. "As the Scriptures say, 'No one is righteous—not even one.

POST CARD

CORRESPONDENCE

Salvation is the spiritual concept of being forgiven of one's sins. Christians believe we are saved through the death and resurrection of Jesus Christ.

Salvación means "salvation."

No one is truly wise; no one is seeking God. All have turned away; all have become useless. No one does good, not a single one. . . . For everyone has sinned; we all fall short of God's glorious standard' (Romans 3:10-12, 23, *NLT*)."

"No one does good, sí, that has been my experience," Shannen's mother noted dryly.

If Mama Cony heard her, she never let on. "The price (or consequence) of sin is death. Romans 6:23 (*NLT*): 'For the wages of sin is death, but the free gift of God is eternal life through Christ Jesus our Lord.' Without Jesus, you will die. And not death, as in escape, but death as in permanent separation from God."

The fan buzzed in the background, but it hardly cut the heat in the room.

Shannen's mother moved slightly backward as Mama Cony pushed her glassed on top of her head and leaned in, "Jesus Christ died for your sin. He paid the price for your death. Romans 5:8 says that 'God showed his great love for us by sending Christ to die for us while we were still sinners.' Isn't that good news? Don't you love the good news?"

Then, to the mother's amazement, the older woman stood up and did a little dance in one spot, spinning around. Shannen stared in wonder. She did not know this woman, but she wanted to hear her talk some more about her good news and about Jesus.

"Here's how this works," Mama Cony sat back down and got very serious. "We receive salvation and eternal life through faith in Jesus Christ. Romans 10:9, 10, and 13 (*NLT*): 'If you confess with your mouth that Jesus is Lord and

All have sinned and fall short of the glory of God.
—Romans 3:23

For the wages of sin is death, but the gift of God is eternal life in Christ Jesus our Lord.
—Romans 3:23

But God demonstrates his own love for us in this: While we were still sinners, Christ died for us.
—Romans 5:8

If you declare with your mouth "Jesus is Lord," and believe in your heart that God raised him from the dead, you will be saved. For it is with your heart that you believe and are justified, and it is with your mouth that you profess your faith and are saved.
—Romans 10:9, 10

Therefore, since we have been justified through faith, we have peace with God through our Lord Jesus Christ.
—Romans 5:1

Therefore, there is now no condemnation for those who are in Christ Jesus.
—Romans 8:1

believe in your heart that God raised him from the dead, you will be saved. For it is by believing in your heart that you are made right with God, and it is by confessing with your mouth that you are saved. For "Everyone who calls on the name of the Lord will be saved.""'

Mama Cony closed her Bible and held out her hand for the young woman's hand. She held her hand gently and looked her straight in the eyes. "Would you like to call on the name of the Lord? Would you like to be saved?" The questions just hung in the air, begging to be answered. Shannen found herself captivated by Mama Cony, with her book and her voice and her questions.

As if listening to a voice only she could hear, the woman cocked her head, and leaned in one final time. "Salvation through Jesus Christ brings us into a relationship of peace with God. Romans 5:1 (*NLT*): 'Therefore, since we have been made right in God's sight by faith, we have peace with God because of what Jesus Christ our Lord has done for us.' Romans 8:1 (*NLT*): 'So now there is no condemnation for those who belong to Christ Jesus.' Do you want peace? Hallelujah! Who wouldn't want peace?" She took a swig of her coffee and observed the two little women over her glasses.

Shannen had sat listening the whole time to Mama Cony, forgetting all about the kitchen set and her new friend. Something about this woman's voice and the feeling she had when Mama Cony was reading . . . her words stilled Shannen. There in the hot office of an orphanage, with the smell of eggs lingering in the air, she felt her need. At the ripe old age of four, she knew that she needed Jesus, and she understood who he could be to her. She wanted peace, she wanted life, and most of all, she wanted love. She closed her eyes and tried to imagine what Jesus looked like.

Mama Cony's voice made her eyes flutter open again. "This is more important than what you came here to do today," she said to Shannen's mother. "Are you ready to pray with me to know this God?"

The woman who woke this morning with the determination to abandon her child in an orphanage nodded, and bowed her head.

But before they could start, Shannen spoke up. "Me too!" Then she folded her hands in her lap and waited.

"Praise you, Jesus," Mama Cony breathed, then prayed with these women for new life to begin.

Later Shannen would describe this memory as her best and worst day. It was the day she said good-bye to her mother, and to the innocent belief that her mother would always be there for her. But it was also the day she said hello to Jesus, and she had been getting to know him every day since.

"That was the day my mom and I accepted Christ. I think that was the perfect moment for us, because we were experiencing a lot of confusion then. My dad had left us, we were bouncing around a lot between houses, staying with 'friends' and feeling unstable. We didn't have any hope, so God came to us that morning as Hope and we said yes to him."

A couple of years after Shannen came to the orphanage, when she was six years old, she began to have dreams—crazy dreams. She would wake up in the girls' dormitory and run to tell Mama Cony. "Jesus was in my dream again! He told me I would bring his Word to the nations! Oh, Mama Cony, I can't imagine!

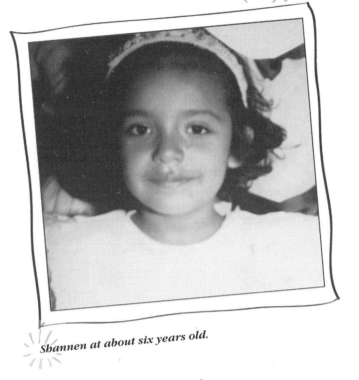

Shannen at about six years old.

How exciting! Do you think it was real? Where are the nations?" Shannen didn't understand all of what was happening, but she was so excited about the feeling stirring inside of her. She felt expectant—like at any moment, something amazing was going to happen.

She grew in those years to love the Jesus in her dreams and in her Bible. She talked to him like a friend and imagined a day when she could serve him.

One morning, after she had woken to a particularly vivid dream, she found Mama Cony in the kitchen. She shared with her that in her dream, she had been very sick, and Jesus had acted like a doctor and healed her.

"There is so much I don't understand." Shannen wound up the end of a towel as she spoke, twisting it tighter and tighter. "I don't know why my mom left me. I don't know why God chose me. I don't know if I am going to get sick, or if I am supposed to pray with someone who is . . . I don't know much . . . so why does God send me these dreams?"

The towel was now in knots. Shannen hung her head and Mama Cony pulled her into a hug. "Let's start with what we do know, and let the rest sort itself out. Now, what do we know?" She looked down at Shannen's face, where tears were traveling down the little girl's cheeks. Mama Cony didn't wait for an answer. "We know you are the daughter of a King, yes? We know that King loves your mom. We know you are forgiven. We know Jesus heals. We know he holds the future . . ."

As Mama Cony recited her list, Shannen lost herself in those thoughts. Her heart calmed. Together, Mama and Shannen ate beans and eggs in silence, thinking about the things that are true of a God neither had ever seen.

Shannen continued to grow in both stature and maturity, and she finished elementary school.

"For I know the plans I have for you," declares the LORD, "plans to prosper you and not to harm you, plans to give you hope and a future."

—Jeremiah 29:11

"What are you writing down?" Mama Cony's daughter came and looked over Shannen's shoulder. Shannen closed her Bible and looked up at her. "Oh! On the back page, I write down all the names of the people I tell about Jesus." She shyly showed her the page, full of names. "I don't know how many of them know him yet, but I won't stop talking about him. I can't, it's inside of me and wants to come out."

The two hugged and prayed over the list of names in Shannen's Bible. *Lord, use this girl for your glory, use her heart, her gifts, her story. Take her to the place where she will learn to lean completely on you. Amen.*

For an orphan's story, Shannen's life had a lot of sunshine in it. Up until she was thirteen, Shannen loved Jesus, loved her family at the children's home, and loved the story she believed was coming in her future. But as she entered adolescence, the questions came. Normally, when she had questions, or even doubts, just listing the truths she knew would chase the clouds away. But in this season, the questions came at her faster than she had answers.

Why am I here? Why am I at a children's home? Why can't I be with my mom? Why don't I have friends like everyone else? If you love me, Lord, why won't you give me what I want? How do people see me? Why can't I see you? How do I know you are real?

So many questions. They were relentless.

As she strained to listen, there were competing voices. Some were voices of truth, and they whispered to her the intense value of her life. Other voices threatened to drown them all, not whispering, but yelling. They shouted with desperation that she needed to take control of her own life. Sometimes the lies sounded right.

There is no one who cares. Look out for yourself.
Take what is yours. If you don't do it, no one will. Do
what feels right. The time is now.

The battle raged on inside of Shannen, and her teenage friends joined the chorus. "Why don't you just leave? What has God ever done for you?" Confusion reigned in this season.

Finally, one day Shannen came home from school, slammed her backpack down on the table, and said, "Enough. I am done! Right now! Call my mom right now. I want to go home. I don't even know what home is, but I want to be there. RIGHT NOW!" She looked around at the room, at the toys scattered on the floor and the well-loved books on the shelf. A little boy and girl sat in the corner. They had been playing a game, but now they just stared at Shannen with big eyes. She could feel her patience fading away, and her anger growing.

"Does anyone hear me?! I am leaving!!"

Another girl came around the corner to see who was making all the noise. "Are we allowed to do that?" she asked the boy in a whisper. "Are we allowed to just tell them when we want to leave?"

"No, I don't think so . . . but it sure sounds like it, doesn't it?" he replied.

Hours later, after many words had been spoken (and some shouted), Shannen's mother showed up at the gate—the same gate where she had come on that early morning so many years ago. Shannen walked out without even saying good-bye to everyone. But as she left, she and the boy who had been sitting in the corner exchanged glances.

He wanted to reach out and touch her arm. He didn't understand what was happening. *What happened to Shannen? What happened to the girl who always read her Bible and shared her amazing dreams?*

"I have to work, you know . . ." Shannen's mom wrung her hands and looked at her angry thirteen-year-old. "I won't be around much, so you'll have to take care of yourself." Her eyes dropped to the floor. "I don't know what you were hoping for, or what you want from me. But I will try to give it to you."

The shame and guilt that had come on her shoulders the day she had left her little girl behind fell on her heavily now. If they had been physical burdens on her back, she would have been crushed to the floor.

She desperately wanted to do something for her daughter—anything. But she already felt defeated. Nothing could take back the pain of that moment when she walked away. As sure as she had known it that morning so long ago, she knew it now. She could not be what Shannen wanted. She could not give her what she needed. She couldn't even tell her the truth.

All she could get out was, "I don't know how long this will work out . . ." Her voice trailed off and she fell silent.

Shannen didn't even hear her mother's words. She was looking around at her home, the place she had spent the first few years of her life. It was mostly filled with her mother's things. She didn't even immediately see any pictures of herself as a child. *No evidence I exist*, Shannen thought. But that was OK. Everything would be different now.

She unpacked her own belongings and started making a corner for herself. This would be her place. Her place, with her things, in her neighborhood. It seemed like a paradise—the freedom, the sense of belonging, the pride of ownership. She would show everyone. *This will work out just fine*, thought Shannen. *I will make sure of it.*

Looking back, Shannen would later say it was that last thought that got her into the most trouble. "I will make sure of it" had an independent sound to it. And that independence bred a defiance that ended up destroying this time in her life.

For almost two years, Shannen and her mom worked at building a life together. Most of the time, Shannen would only see her mom on Sundays. The rest of the week, her mother worked until late in the night and would come home after Shannen was already asleep. Shannen made herself meals, asked herself her homework questions, and told herself to clean up. She was in every way raising herself. At the very beginning, that felt wonderful and free. But very soon, Shannen found this way of life to be extremely lonely. She was used to a dorm full of friends and Mama Cony and the rest of the children's staff. At the children's home, there had always been someone to talk to. Here she could only talk to herself.

As a result of that loneliness, Shannen almost immediately made poor choices in friends. She felt drawn to anyone who would show her any attention whatsoever.

After school, she would come home and do her homework. Then she would fix herself some small meal. Occasionally, she would clean up the kitchen and tidy up the other rooms. She tried on purpose to do all of these things slowly, filling the time remaining before bedtime. Then at night, she would tell herself she was too tired to read her Bible. But the reality was, she just didn't want to hear that voice any longer.

Her new lifestyle left her feeling bored and apathetic. "I just want to feel normal. I don't know, is this what normal feels like?" she asked a new friend in the park near her home one day.

Her friend Angelica kicked a pebble down the path and then answered. "Yeah, feels pretty normal

POST CARD

CORRESPONDENCE

Entumecido means "numb."

to me. Nothing to do. Nowhere to go. No idea what's next. *Entumecido*. That's how I have always felt."

Something stirred inside Shannen. *This is* not *how I have always felt.* She knew that this was her opening to talk to her friend about Jesus. But the words got stuck inside her throat. *What is wrong with me? I have done this 100 times!* But try as she might, she couldn't remember the verse in Romans that always got her started. Something was terribly wrong. *What am I doing? Where am I? Who am I?*

Shannen's mother woke up on Sunday morning and pulled herself out of bed. It had seemed like an especially long week of work, and she was tired down to her bones. She wrapped a robe around her and shuffled into the kitchen to put on a pot of coffee. She was surprised to find Shannen already there.

"*Buenos días*, Mama. I made coffee for you." Shannen poured some into a cup and handed it to her mother.

"*Gracias*," her mother replied. It had been hard having Shannen living with her. She had to make many adjustments that Shannen didn't even have any idea about. But she had to admit it felt good just having someone in the house with her. The house didn't seem so lonely now. And to wake up to the smell of coffee already brewing! Well, that was just really nice.

However, in the past few weeks, even though she didn't see her much, she had felt Shannen becoming more and more restless. *Perhaps I have some motherly sensibilities after all*, she thought.

"Mama, I've been wanting to talk to you," Shannen began. "I don't feel right. Something is making me very antsy. I'm not happy here."

Her mom shook her head. "Shannen, I don't understand you. I don't know what you need. I don't have anything else for you. This is it." She waved her arm around the kitchen. "I am not very good at this and I never pretended to be. I don't know if I can help you. What is it that you want?"

POST CARD

CORRESPONDENCE

**Buenos dias means "Good morning."
Gracias means "thank you."**

What do I want? She thought about this on the way to school the next day.

What do I want? She thought when the teacher handed her back another test she had failed.

What do I want? She thought later that day when her boyfriend pressured her for more than she was willing to give.

What do I want? And she wondered who she was even talking to.

"No, Mama, I won't go back! This time you can't trick me or make me. I'm too big for that now."

After receiving a report about Shannen's failing grades that week, her mother knew this situation could not continue. It wasn't good for Shannen. If she really wanted to throw away any chance she had at making a life for herself, well, she wasn't going to be able to stop her. But she also didn't want to be responsible for it. She couldn't stand any more guilt.

So over lunch that Sunday, she had carefully brought up the idea of Shannen going back to the children's home. She tried to reason with her daughter. She tried talking about her future.

"Do you want to end up like me? Working all the time just to get barely get by. Just to come home to nothing?"

"Not nothing—I'm here. I have freedom here. I have you here." The tears started coming faster now. Eleven years of bitterness and anger and sorrow and longing filled up her heart and poured out in sharp, biting words. "Don't you want me? Are you going to get rid of me again? Really? Really?? What are you going to do, Mama? What lie will you tell me this time? What game will we play? How are you going to get me to go?"

Shannen's mother looked into her daughter's accusing eyes and said nothing. What could she say? She felt like a failure all over again.

The tension in the room was suffocating. Shannen grabbed her jacket and slammed the front door behind her as she struck out for the park.

Shannen took a different route to the park than normal, hoping to avoid any familiar faces along the way. She didn't want to talk to anyone right now. In the silence, her own words to her mother echoed in her head and she felt horrible. She didn't want to hurt her mother.

She could feel the Spirit stirring inside of her, but

it had been so long, she didn't feel comfortable with it. "What do you want from me?" she spoke into the air.

She felt like a horse being broken and refusing to bend to the will of her trainer. She stomped around the park all the rest of that afternoon, walking in circles, speaking to herself, crying, shouting, and finally, sitting quietly. The sun was setting and the moon had come out. She knew she ought to go home, but wasn't even sure where that was anymore. Was it the children's home? Her mother's house? Her friend's home? With her boyfriend?

Where do I belong?

In the morning, Shannen's mother woke up again to a surprise. Even though it was very early, Shannen sat at the kitchen table, dressed and ready to go. Her mother noticed the packed bag sitting beside her on the floor.

"Mama, it's time to go."

They both knew what she meant.

Shannen's mother nodded. She looked around the few small rooms, checking to see if Shannen had forgotten anything. Then she grabbed her purse and held out her hand to her daughter.

Although every part of her screamed during the familiar bus ride back to the children's home, she knew down deep inside that God was taking care of her in that moment. He had spent her lifetime protecting her from others and now he was guarding her from herself. She would later say that even though she didn't want to go back, she knew it was God calling her to finish his purpose.

"Welcome home, *hija*," was all Mama Cony said, when she saw the dejected expression on Shannen's face. She opened her arms and Shannen buried herself in the familiar scent. She looked around for other faces she knew and saw a few. She cried all the way up the stairs and into the girls' dorm. She cried when she looked over at her old bunk, now filled

POST CARD

Hija means "daughter."

with the belongings of someone else, and she cried when someone told her the bell would ring shortly for dinner.

Really, Lord? Was this necessary? She cried out to Jesus, being in this place already made it easier to do so. *What could you possibly still have for me here?*

"Well, you have made a mess of things haven't you?" Mama Cony had always been a truth teller. She settled in at the foot of Shannen's bed later that night for a heart-to-heart with the girl. "Bad grades—I hope they take you back at this school. Bad attitude—I hope that comes around sooner versus later. What else? Tell me what else we are dealing with here, and don't hold back. I need to know everything if we are going to get you back on track."

There was something about Mama Cony's voice, her holy confidence, and this shelter that broke Shannen. "I am hurt. Terribly hurt. I am angry and disappointed. I wanted something more and instead found something less." She poured out her heart and told of the false friends and bad boys. She shared about her loneliness and her absentee mother.

"Of course you found something less, you looked for life outside of Jesus. You know that verse, John 10:10, says, "The thief comes only to steal, kill and destroy; I have come that they may have life . . .""

"—and have it to the full!" Shannen finished the verse and smiled at Mama Cony. She wasn't sure what else she believed in at the moment, but she knew she believed in Mama Cony and she thought those words sounded more real than any others she had heard lately.

It always starts that way. First we like a person, then the person acts as a bridge to the Savior. And the Savior does all the rest.

Shannen knew that, and had been that person for others. But now it was her that was waiting for "all the rest." *Come Jesus, come back to me. Bring me life. Whatever life is, I want to taste it again. This taste in my mouth is bitter. Bring me your sweet again.*

As the year passed, Shannen's heart was like a plant desperately in need of water. As she came to the source of Living Water, the plant came back to life.

"Felicidades!" Shannen moved around the room, thanking the kids who threw her and her roommates a graduation party. She had finally finished ninth grade and it was the end of an era. Her time at the children's home was over, just as she was appreciating again all the shelter it offered.

Now, as before, she had two choices before her. Ninth grade was the end of mandatory education in Mexico, a natural time for orphans to return to extended family and offer their help in supporting the family unit. She could go back to her mother's house, which was now a terrifying idea to her. Her mother hadn't issued an invitation, and they both knew it would be no better this time than it was the last. But there was more to it than that. As some of her friends prepared to go back home to become caregivers for their mother's next round of children, or for an aging grandparent, or to try and make a life together with a boyfriend, she knew she wanted something more.

Her other option was to enroll in high school with a select group of other children from orphanages around the city at a ministry called Back2Back Ministries. There they were offering her an opportunity to continue her studies while living in a Christian environment. Although this second option would open up many doors for her future and make her the most educated member of her family, it made her nervous.

More school? More expectation? More rules? Lord, are you sure? What if I don't have what it

From Beth's Journal

In many of these stories, we see how the Storyweaver places people in our lives to help us in ways we never could have known at the time. In Shannen's case, her "helper" was the least likely candidate—the mother who had abandoned her. But it was only through her time with her mother and through experiencing both abandonment and abandoning, that Shannen came to understand the peace and grace and purpose she had been looking for. Sometimes God works through our hurts and even through those who hurt us to bring about great good. As Joseph said to his brothers, "You intended to harm me, but God meant it for good."

takes? What if it's lonely? What if I don't succeed? I sense you leading me there, but I am so scared. What if I can't do it?

The quiet voice came to her, familiar and comforting, *More opportunity, more growth, more of Me, more to the story . . .*

Shannen sighed. He was right, of course. It was a step of faith, but on solid ground. If God was leading her, then it was for a good purpose. Hearing his voice felt better than she'd ever imagined. She was walking in the Spirit again.

Shannen completed all three years of high school. She graduated in 2013 and now is a nursing student at a fine university. Throughout her high school education, she spent her vacations going to orphanages in other cities, telling them the story of Jesus and his good news for us all.

As I (Beth) write this, Shannen has a plane ticket to travel to Haiti this year and share with the thousands of orphans there about a Savior who wants more than just eternal life with us—he wants daily life with us.

As the plans came together for this trip, Shannen shared with me excitedly, "I am going to the nations. Just as Jesus promised in my childhood dreams. My history doesn't define me, instead it empowers me to tell the story of a Father who never lets go. I can't wait to share with the Haitian orphans biblical truths. This is my story. This is our God. And this is what it feels like to be swept up into a dream. Praise you, Jesus!"

"For I am convinced that neither death nor life, neither angels nor demons, neither the present nor the future, nor any powers, neither height nor depth, nor anything else in all creation, will be able to separate us from the love of God that is in Christ Jesus our Lord" (Romans 8:38, 39).

Has something ever come between you and your faith in Christ? What happened? What do you think of the verses above?

Do you, like Shannen, have a dream to serve God? What is it? Write your thoughts here.

Chapter 6

TURNING THE PAGES

As I write this chapter, I am on an airplane, heading to another country where I will spend a few days hugging as many kids as I can. Some people may ask if I think a few days will really make a difference. I think that every day is a day that we have a chance to be God's hands and feet. So yes, every day makes a difference. I don't know who God asked to hug these kids last week or when I will be back for another round. I just know that I am not in charge. I am to listen and obey.

He is the Master Leader-Outer. He is the One who sees all the characters in the story. He is the One who has written our names in the palm of his hand (Isaiah 49).

When God prompts you to reach out to a neighbor or someone in your class or sporting team or music school, don't talk yourself out of it. That's what we do all the time. *I am too busy. They won't*

understand me. I am afraid. It won't make any dif-
ference. Those are lies, and believing them can stop
us from being part of some of the best stories.

Stories like that of Priyanka and her sisters, who
are still today living their stories out in India. Have
you found that country on the map yet? Have you
ever met anyone from India? If not, then now you
have! Priyanka would like you to pray for them, and
for the chapters yet to come. She is exercising her
faith muscle and waiting to see how God answers her
request to see her father again.

God always answers our prayers. Sometimes
exactly what we are hoping for is his delight to
deliver. Other times, what we are asking for doesn't
align with his perfect will. If we could see all that he
sees, we would fully understand. The Bible teaches
us that today we see in part, but one day we'll see the
whole. When your partial vision causes you to doubt
God's plan, stop and remind yourself what you know
to be true: He loves you. He has a plan. He sees from
the beginning to the end.

Even though she may live on the other side of the world from you and have a very different life from yours, it's likely that you've had some of the same questions Priyanka has had. Is there some unexplained mystery in your family's story? Are there broken relationships that haven't been mended? Do you ever worry about what your future will look like? Perhaps you live in a single-parent home, or have younger siblings you look out for. Keep turning the pages of any person's story, and you will find common threads. Keep turning the pages of God's story and you will eventually find answers.

Imagine what would have happened if Melanie had not stepped forward for Adrian. What if she had allowed others to tell her she couldn't make a difference? What if she had believed that, since she didn't speak his language or live nearby, there was no hope for a real relationship? Think of how rich Adrian and Melanie's lives are now, how neither of them could imagine life without the other. I've said it before and I'll say it here again: God writes the best stories.

Who do you think God might be asking you to reach out to? What thoughts stop you? I wonder (and we'll never know) whose life is different today because Adrian has grown to understand what he has to offer. That's what's so amazing to me, this ripple effect. When you reach out and love someone in the name of Jesus, that deposit has a way of overflowing into more lives. You set off a chain reaction. Only in Heaven will we see all the ways God has used our obedience.

I have some friends in Mexico who grew up in children's homes. They are orphans who are studying at the university level. They have decided between themselves that they want to take the hope God has given them (for a future and a family and a life and a story bigger than them) to another country. They listened and heard God whisper: Haiti. They want to invest their stories in people who don't speak their language and have skin of a different color, but who share the same hope for healing. Watching them prepare for this holy assignment has been like seeing a living example of this spiritual principle I am talking about. We can allow the Lord to fill us, then we can spill what he has provided over onto others.

Anne-Marie is a comedian. She is hilarious and spends much of her time cracking up the rest of the children at the Lighthouse. There is so much joy in her heart. She just turned ten and that meant she could finally join the Power Girls, a group of preteen and teen girls who meet together to talk about God's Word. This year, she had a summer challenge of writing out the entire book of John. Each night she carefully copied the words from the Bible into her journal. When she got to John 10, she read: "The gate-keeper opens the gate for him, and the sheep listen to his voice. He calls his own sheep by name and leads them out."

She ran to find one of the staff at the home. "Listen! I am writing down John for Kristi's Power Girls Challenge. This is the verse I just wrote down and it's the one Derson first read to me, almost a year ago now. I didn't understand it at the time, but now I think I do. I am the sheep, right? I listen for his voice. I have a name and he calls me by it. Isn't that right?"

The care worker patiently replied, "Yes, that's right. He is revealing to you this ancient promise. But don't forget the last part; it's powerful and your life is a testimony to its truth. 'He leads them out.'"

Anne-Marie and Derson both know what it means to be led out of an impossible situation. They know God is writing every detail of their lives. And as we turn the pages of his book, we can find wisdom for the pages of our own stories.

You met Steve from Kenya, whose story also continues. God brings perfect strangers into his home, something God has been doing since Moses was put into a reed basket and sent into the arms of a princess. We read in the Bible that "God sets the lonely in families" (Psalms 68:6). Sometimes that means a permanent family, other times it means a place of belonging, for however long it's needed.

Recently, while talking to some Back2Back Ministries staff who also live in Africa, I learned of an orphanage that takes in sick children. The Nigerian director told me of a girl named Patience. In the director's own words, she wrote this:

I love the testimony of one of the older girls, Patience. I love her smile, still there despite that at fifteen, she entered first grade due to her illiteracy. She was very shy and very defensive. Patience would complain all the time and didn't want to be called upon to answer a question or even introduce herself. She cried when corrected. It was an overwhelming experience and I know it was a hard time for her; looking back, I don't know how she overcame her fears and confusion.

Can you imagine how that felt for her? A fifteen-year-old going to first grade, not having a family, living with strangers who spoke another language and who were correcting her on behavior no one had ever told her was wrong? Her letter to me continues:

A few days ago while in her class, I asked Patience to read. I was overwhelmed with emotion when she slowly but accurately began to read the words on the page. She has become helpful and doesn't complain as much as she used to. She is in the transformational process and it's a joy to witness a child who comes in afraid (filled with grief and sorrow), but in a short while develops confidence and strength to face the future. How many teenage girls like Patience will have an opportunity to go to school and escape the cycle of violence, poverty, and disease?

Patience's whole life is being changed, because someone decided to stick around when she had a bad attitude and wasn't appreciative. That stick-with-it-ness is exactly what we all need a little more of these days. It's what has led Steve to offer his home up to boys who need security and love. Reaching out once is still a challenge, but reaching out and loving over and over and over again is what will make the difference in the lives of these children.

I've already told you about Shannen, and how she is going to fulfill her dream of taking Jesus to the nations. Shannen is a friend of mine. I care about her story and her future, and it was my pleasure to introduce you to her. As amazing as Shannen is though, another hero in that story is Mama Cony. Mama Cony put someone else's needs above her own. She listened to a Shepherd who whispered to her to take the hand of this lost sheep and lead her out. Mama Cony is a force—a big love force that won't accept defeat and loves at great cost to herself. She has walked with God so long and so well, you know she recognizes his voice.

She can tell you story after story of children like Shannen, who she loved into the kingdom and then through the plotlines of their lives.

As I finish the third book in the Storyweaver series, I am convinced of this: God wants us to participate with him in this redemptive work. He is looking for us to be his agents, to be his hands and feet. As you look around today, ask him for his eyes, his heart, and his courage to see and love and speak out to a world that is lost and wondering if God even notices. Ask him for the wisdom of Steve and Goldie and Tom and Mama Cony and Melanie . . . Ask him to write you into one of his tales.

Beth wrote her first book in third grade. It was about a frog. Mrs. Pate may never have liked it, but her mother still takes it out and looks at it occasionally. Since then, Beth has written other books, such as *Reckless Faith* (Zondervan, 2008), *Relentless Hope* (Standard Publishing, 2011), *Tales of the Not Forgotten* (Standard Publishing, 2012), and *Tales of the Defended Ones* (Standard Publishing, 2013).

Beth has a houseful of kids—there are some in elementary, a couple in junior high, a high-schooler, a few college students, and two who live independently now. Besides her family, Beth likes all forms of chocolate, the ocean in any season, traveling, and Christmastime.

Beth met her husband, Todd, at age seventeen at Young Life Bible study. She knew she liked him when he offered her one of his three versions of the Bible (since she had forgotten hers). Together they have spent seventeen years on the mission field and continue to work together with Back2Back Ministries to bring care for today and hope for tomorrow to orphans around the world.

Acknowledgments

Every book is a team effort! Here are the principle players in the *Tales of the Ones Led Out* team.

Thank you to Toni, Kristi, and Jenna for helping me gather details for the stories. The people we are privileged to have as a part of the Back2Back Ministries family always bless me.

Thank you to Stephanie, Matt, Lindsay, Laura, and Bob from Standard for believing in these stories and working hard to get them out there. It's been a fun journey as we endeavor to engage the next generation.

Thank you to the Back2Back Ministries team, who live these stories with me each and every day. You all stun me with your obedience, authenticity, and vulnerability. I love serving alongside of you.

Thank you to my family, who are patient when I need to go over the stories one more time and who share in our family adventures. I love God's plan for the Guckenbergers.

And to my Mom, who instilled in me a love of reading, of God's ways and of children. Your investment in me is something I appreciate every day!

HOW IS GOD WEAVING YOUR STORY?

"Our hope with this curriculum is to esource churches to help open kids' eyes the needs in their community and around e world. I believe we have the opportunity to invest in this next generation, to show them how God sees the lost and the fatherless, and to help kids understand ow He wants to use them! We believe that y inspiring kids through true stories, they ill begin to make a personal contribution to caring for orphans around the world."

Beth Guckenberger,

Executive Director of Back2Back Ministries

www.back2back.org

These powerful stories of God's work in the lives of poor and abandoned kids will inspire kids to get involved in missions.

Beth Guckenberger, Executive Director of Back2Back Ministries and author of *Tales of the Not Forgotten*, *Tales of the Defended Ones* and now *Tales of the Ones Led Out* shares a collection of unforgettable, real stories in each of these amazing books. Help your kids connect their lives with the stories of children around the world with the interactive leader's guides available online or on CD-ROM.

Leader's Guide
025485112 • $7.99

Leader's Guide
025495213 • $7.99

025495113 • $8.99

025485212 • $8.99

My name is ALONDRA.

I love to swim and listen to music. I like math and want to be a teacher when I grow up.

Alondra is a confident eight-year-old, full of laughter and curiosity. Her favorite color is purple, she has two siblings, and she has lived in an orphanage for as long as she can remember. Each morning, she wakes up in a dormitory full of other girls and walks to school. In the evening, she does her homework and chores before going to bed.

Alondra is just one of 163 million orphaned children in our world. But unlike many other orphans, Alondra will wake up tomorrow knowing she's loved by her Father God. She will see God's love through her good meals, through her tutor after school, through her houseparents who care for her daily, through the visiting families who come to play with her, and through the Back2Back staff who hold her hand at church. Alondra may be physically orphaned, but she is wonderfully loved.

My name is Daniel.

I like to play soccer and climb the rocks behind my house. My favorite subject is English.

Daniel lives in Jos, Nigeria, where he attends Back2Back's Education Center. At the center, he has good meals, care when he is sick, and a safe place to learn.

When Daniel first came to the Education Center, he was very shy. He rarely laughed or smiled. But now, through the love and attention of Back2Back staff, he has grown to become a confident boy, full of laughter and joy.

Daniel hopes to be a teacher when he grows up. For the first time in his life, Daniel is thriving and well on his way to reaching his goals for a brighter tomorrow.

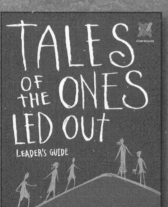